RISE

QUEER SCI FI'S TENTH ANNUAL FLASH FICTION
CONTEST

Published by
Other Worlds Ink
PO Box 19341, Sacramento, CA 95819

❀ Created with Vellum

CONTENTS

PARANORMAL PART ONE

FANTASY PART TWO

SCIENCE FICTION PART TWO

HORROR

FANTASY PART THREE

SCIENCE FICTION PART THREE

PARANORMAL PART TWO

FANTASY PART FOUR

FOREWORD

It's hard to tell a story in just 300 words, so it's only fair that I limit this foreword to exactly 300 words, too. This year, 454 writers took the challenge, with stories across the queer spectrum. The contest rules are simple. Submit a complete, well-written themed 300 word sci-fi, fantasy, paranormal or horror story with LGBTQ+ characters.

For our tenth year and ninth anthology, we chose the theme "Rise." The interpretations run from rising bread to zombies rising from the grave, from sunrise to rising on feathered wings. There are little jokes, big surprises, and future prognostications that will make your head spin.

I'm proud that this collection includes many colors of the LGBTQ+ (or QUILTBAG, if you prefer) universe—lesbian, gay, bisexual, transgender, intersex, queer, and asexual characters populate these pages—our most diverse contest yet. There's a bit of romance, too—and a number of stories solidly on the "mainstream" side. Flash fiction is short, fun, and easy to read. You may not fall in love with every story—in fact, you probably won't. But if you don't like one, just move on to the next, and you're sure to find some bite-sized morsels of flash fiction goodness. There are so many good stories in here—choose your own favorites.

We chose three winning stories, five judges' choice picks, and two director's picks, all marked in the text. Thanks to our judges—Angel Martinez, Ben Lilley, Sacchi Green, Lloyd Meeker, and Diane Allen—for selflessly giving their time, love, and energy to this project. And to Ryane Candyce too, for editing.

At Queer Sci Fi, we're building a community of writers and readers who want a little rainbow in their speculative fiction. Join us and submit a story of your own next time!

FANTASY PART ONE

It tasted like honeysuckle and lilacs, the first breath after I died.

Why do the branches look so much like roots? Why do my lungs look so much like the branches? I exhaled through the question like air rustling through leaves. Back taut on the dirt, the Earth's gravity rose and fell on my chest.

— M EDGETTE, DIONYSUS' GARDEN

RISE UP
NATHAN ALLING LONG (300 WORDS)

Director's Choice - J. Scott Coatsworth

We lived in a queer collective house. From our upstairs window, we could see past the abandoned lot to the park on the corner—until they built the apartments in-between us.

At first we looked down in fascination, watching the bulldozer level land, the shirtless workmen digging trenches in summer.

When they put up the scaffolding, Petunia declared, "There goes our view."

"And our privacy," Tomboy added.

Floor after floor, it rose, looming over our house.

"It's like a big hard on," Rover said, and we all laughed.

Every morning, we'd see workers board the elevator. All day, we'd hear drills and hammers. At dusk, they'd spill out onto the street.

Soon it shadowed our entire vegetable garden.

"Is there no limit?" Birdie said. "No ordinances?"

By autumn, we couldn't even see the top.

Still they built.

₰

THEN ONE DAY in late Spring, we heard creaking. The building began to sway. It was leaning over our collective house. The creaking turned to groaning. The building bent further and further, until the upper floors stretched over our property, hovering above the neighbor's yard.

"It's going to fall," Sasha said, running into the street.

We watched it bend down slowly over our roof, like a giant slinky, touching down on the other side.

Then, somewhere in the middle, right over our house, the building began to split in two, without spilling a brick.

Once it separated, the two sides straightened up. A tower now stood on either side of us.

We were horrified and relieved: at least, our house was saved.

The next day, men came and piled into both buildings with tools and supplies.

Again, the buildings rose.

We knew what was coming: they'd soon multiply in some new direction, slowly taking over the neighborhood, blocking our sun, squeezing us out.

The competition for Director's Choice was especially fierce this year. In the end, it came down to three that I absolutely loved. I whittled it down to two, and am exercising my prerogative again to name both of those stories as this year's "choice." This one, as it was utterly unique among all the stories submitted. The "Slinky" aspect reminded me of my childhood, and the subject matter tapped into very current worries about the direction of our cities. And the author managed it all with style and a distinctly queer flavor. I loved this darkly whimsical tale.

—J. Scott Coatsworth

DIONYSUS' GARDEN
MARKUS MCCANN EDGETTE (294 WORDS)

It tasted like honeysuckle and lilacs, the first breath after I died.

Why do the branches look so much like roots? Why do my lungs look so much like the branches? I exhaled through the question like air rustling through leaves. Back taut on the dirt, the Earth's gravity rose and fell on my chest.

Will it go black? I catastrophized, *not yet, not yet, not yet!* I could still feel the warmth of his mouth on my neck, the strength of her fingers entwined in mine. It ached more like desire than a memory. *Will they know I'm gone, my loves? Was I ever...really there?*

The question was a staggering blow, the kind of statement that led to a radical shift, like "Do I believe in God?" or "Why don't I feel like a boy?" or "Am I gay?"

Why do the roots look so much like the branches?

The crunch of a shovel whacked distantly, dwarfed by a melody, a melody that whistled and warbled its way from shrills to muted harmony. My eyes fell closed, embraced a dull absence to settle into opiate oneness with interwoven birdsongs. Cool tears perched on my damp lashes, *Was I ever really there?*

"No." An audible voice answered my silent question.

My eyes shot open; twitters plunged deep in my stomach.

His strong olive hands gently lifted my chin. Face to foliate face The Green Man touched his furrowed oak brow to mine and cradled my cold cheek, "You weren't there. You *are* there. Every rapture, every joy, you are my joy. This place is possibility" he smiled, "it's a place that we're building for you."

I choked on a sob.

Darkness.

It tasted like honeysuckle and lilacs, the first breath after I was born.

RETURNED TO LIFE
JAIME MUNN (300 WORDS)

Honorable Mention

There are traces here; just not divine. Instinct says nature spirit, a *vetter*. Not what they're paying for. I should move to the next site, but the air is full of lonely. Something I'm heart-deep in. I feel it like a punch through me, pulling on empathy strings.

I linger. Brushing the silky faux buzz cut—an anxious tick—hugging a deformed chest that doesn't feel like mine, reluctant to submit to emotional blackmail.

Energy and time I won't get back, can't charge for. Life's too short!

Then there's a hit of perfume; a fruity note that screams pomegranate and I'm hooked. My name isn't Persephone, but the underworld has my number.

"Fuck it," I say, slamming the car door, approaching the centre of the manifestation. It feels like a gentle caress. That's never a solid clue. I've had soft turn dangerously hard in the past. "What are you?"

The faded spirit can't answer. Not yet. I walk the edges of the haunting, tracing an energy corral round the remnants, before standing to the East like a rising sun. My aura flickers with dark spots and I flinch. Even when 'all clear' rings through my thoughts, I still imagine the cancer sleeps inside. I push fear away, draw on my wounded strength, and re-coalesce the spirit.

It starts. A clouded jewel in the air, heatwave distortions. Then transmutes into a beautiful woman—indigo eyes and white hair—hovering between earth and sky. A sylphid.

Her cool gaze is sensual as I break the energy ring confining her, but she vanishes without a thank you. It hurts.

In the car, I glance into the rear-view mirror; looking like G.I. Jane but paler, still jinxed by sickly. Alone. Until, beyond my reflection... sylph eyes. Our flirting is mutual and the backseat inviting.

THE DARKEST NIGHT

C.J. SCOTT (298 WORDS)

"If you are not back before sunrise, the spell cannot be undone."
I am sprinting through the woods in a t-shirt that falls to my knees. Somewhere on the trail behind me, my boots lay abandoned alongside my pants and boxers. In hindsight, it's obvious that the transformation would only affect me – not my wardrobe. If I had thought this through, I would have brought a change of clothes.

If I had thought this through, I wouldn't have made a deal with a witch.

What choice did I have? Mother is ill; nothing is helping. Father made me promise to care for her and my sisters when he died. I am the man of the house; I must protect them.

I arrive at the lake breathless. The Moon hovers overhead, full and perfectly reflected on the silent water below–two glowing eyes, watching my approach.

"One does not simply trick the Moon."
I push the witch's warning from my mind, close my eyes, and plunge into the lake. The water reaches out to me as I break the surface, grasps me with cold hands, drags me down. My ears pop. My lungs scream.

The Moon knows. I am no woman. She will not let me leave this lake with a moonstone for the witch. She sees through the spell and—

There is something in my hand. Next thing I know, I have dragged myself to shore. I hold the smooth, translucent gem in front of me, laughing in disbelief. My reflection laughs alongside me, and I freeze.

Dark waves of hair cling to a face I recognize as mine. But it is softer, more graceful.

I am beautiful.

"If you are not back before sunrise, the spell cannot be undone."
I set the moonstone beside me and wait.

RAIN.

RJ MUSTAFA (300 WORDS)

A fresh moon crescent peeked, complicit, as man and spirit said their goodbyes.

Parched, lifeless earth crackled under their dust-stained sandals. They held each other so tightly that they would crumble, surely, if they broke their embrace. From deep within his chest, Eli hummed as he wiped his lover's tears. Words couldn't voice the depth of his grief, so he crashed his lips against his in a fury.

I love you. Let the world desiccate and stay with me. Let me die in your stead.

Why wasn't Eli screaming all those things? He wanted to lift him up in his slender arms and flee, somewhere drought and duty did not exist. Where there was only him and Raim, their love sheltering them in warm solitude.

"I will keep your memory alive," Eli whispered instead, laying his head on the spirit's shoulder. Eli felt him wavering, as the magic ached to leave his body and return to its source.

Raim's tears rolled sweetness over his tongue. He smelled of the baobab oil they'd rubbed their skin with—protection against scorching winds. Gold began shimmering over Raim's skin and from within the feathers tattooed over his clavicles. The spirit squeezed Eli's hand. He took in the sight of his lover's sharp eyes, indigo-black skin, long fingers that never left him without touch...

"In another world, I would be yours, entirely," Raim replied in a fractured voice. He left a dying kiss on Eli's forehead, before bursting into a thousand gold and cerulean sprinkles.

There was no voice to cover the sound of the man's heart shattering.

Instead, he stared as they fused into the large, ethereal bird that would bring the water back.

It shrieked, soaring toward the heavens. Then the rain came, cold and ardent, drowning the last of Eli's tears.

WHERE DOES MAGIC COME FROM?

CHISTO HEALY (300 WORDS)

Honorable Mention

Declan stared out at the crowd. Sweat beaded on his forehead, his hands were clammy. It was hard to breathe. They were all staring, all waiting. He swallowed a lump in his throat and scratched the back of his neck.

"You know the rules," said the Arch-Mage. "You have reached your eighteenth year, Declan, yet you show no signs of magic. If you do not discover your power by adulthood, you must be banished from the guild, never to return. This is your last chance."

"I'm trying." Declan licked his lips nervously. He tried not to see the whole crowd, to focus on one person who looked back at him, equally anxious. Declan nodded. He put his hands out, palms to the ground, and concentrated, but nothing happened.

"You must levitate," said the Arch-Mage. "Rise, boy!" His voice commanded, his elderly face twisted by anger. "Now!"

"I'm trying," Declan said weakly. He found his strength out there among the onlookers again. Then he closed his eyes and took a slow, deep breath.

"What are you doing? You're distracted. This is no time for girls and folly, boy. You stand to be banished."

Declan's eyes opened. He spoke more confidently. "That's just it. I can't access my power because it's stuffed down. I'm stuffed down, hidden."

He looked out towards the one again and waved them towards the stage.

"What is the meaning of this?" barked the Arch-Mage.

"Freedom," said Declan. He smiled at the young man that ran up to him, taking his hands in his own.

"Are you sure?" said the other man nervously.

"Surest I've ever been," Declan told him.

"This is ridiculous. I should banish you both!"

Declan kissed his love, and together they rose, above the stage, above the crowd, above judgment. Declan found his magic.

NEVER SAY DIE

NIA QUINN (295 WORDS)

Three hours into my ritual beneath the new moon, and five hours after I'd started desecrating the grave before me, I lit a freeze-dried raccoon placenta on fire with a spark at the tip of my finger. I chucked it atop the coffin at the bottom of the hole.

Hopefully the damn box wouldn't catch fire this time.

Oh, untwist your knickers already—no raccoons were harmed in the making of this necromantic ritual.

Flames faded to smoking embers. A thump echoed within the coffin, then a muffled, "Crap."

The lid eased upward, scattering the dirt I'd been too unmotivated to bother with. Thank Marsha they didn't nail coffins shut these days—I lost my crowbar at that minotaur brawl last summer.

Tully got to their feet, skinny as ever and only mostly dead-looking in their punk-rock tux.

"Again, Nova, really? Don't they say to let sleeping dogs lie?"

"You're not *that* much of a dog." I helped them out of the grave.

"You're just being nice because I was dead five minutes ago. Seriously, I appreciate the effort, but you've gotta let me go next time, 'kay? How many thousands have you spent on kraken ink by now?"

"Eh, so I'm in debt. What's new? Besides, this is easier than making another friend." I grinned. "With benefits."

Tully took in the elaborate ritual setup. "Define *making*. Because pretty much anything seems easier than this, even for a demi. Heard of Franken-stein's monster?"

I linked arms with Tully, dislodging grave dirt from their sleeve. "Just come home with me already, party pooper. Doctor Who's back on tomorrow, plus Queen Flouncems misses you."

"That cat hates me, and you know it."

"Whatever."

Tully kicked the coffin shut behind us, and we headed home, arm in arm.

NECROMANCING BUBBA

W. DALE JORDAN (297 WORDS)

Honorable Mention

Coy lifted the lid on the coffin and stared at Bubba, his husband who died only days before. In a fit of grief, Coy had visited the old hag Marceline, and begged for a spell to bring Bubba back. Marceline came through, writing the words she said would do the trick.

"Dig him up first," she'd said. "It's rude to make 'em fight to the surface. Pisses 'em off. You be careful, Coy Wallace. You screw up. That's on you."

Coy pushed himself to his feet and rechecked the paper before lifting his hands to the sky.

"God of Death, I beseech you to raise this man who I love. Fill his lungs with air and set his heart to beating."

Didn't sound like a spell, but what did he know?

Coy stared down at his husband. When nothing happened, he read it again. And again and again, until his grief turned to rage.

"Screw you, you bastard; give me what I want, damn it. I said the words the witch gave me. If you can't do this one little thing, you ain't no real god!"

He fell to his knees and shook the coffin, then leaned in when Bubba's face twitched.

"I'll be damned," he said when Bubba's eyes opened.

"What did you do?" Bubba asked.

"I brought you back, baby. I love you. Aren't you happy?"

"I love you, too, but you screwed the pooch, Coy. You and your mouth."

"What do you mean?"

17

Bubba didn't have to answer. Around them the earth shook. Graves burst open. Hands reached for the sky.

All the dead were rising and worse, they were looking at him, reaching for him. Seconds later, he swore he heard laughter in a roll of thunder above them.

"Oh," Coy said. "Well...shit."

DO PAINT THE MEADOWS WITH DELIGHT

JEFF BAKER (255 WORDS)

Honorable Mention

Auris sighed as she eyed their garden glumly.

The gray skies had brought rain but no flowers. The row of plants at the back of the house stubbornly refused to grow, let alone bloom.

Marac would be returning soon after her two weeks away from the house they called "Love Cottage." Two weeks of what she described as "a boring gaggle of Sorcerers and acolytes of the Dal Lords, learning nothing but talking a lot."

Auris stayed home, maintained the house and the garden. Not that the garden looked maintained.

The garden looked like winter.

It was a small strip of ground right next to the house, but it was still theirs.

She heard a noise; Marac returning. Auris raised her hands and spoke.

"Harka, I, through all the Dal

Rise ye flowers, straight and tall."

It didn't quite rhyme, she reflected. 'Dal' usually rhymed with 'pal,' so 'tall should be pronounced...wait...

Something was happening. The little green shoots were stirring as if blown by a breeze. But there was no breeze.

In another moment the green shoots were ripped out of the ground and rose, hovering in the air. Still not blooming.

Then Marac walked up, and all Auris could see was her flowing hair and a dusty travel cloak. Her wife's dusty cloak looked elegant to Auris.

They kissed, eyes closed in the spring sunshine.

The flecks of dirt from the hovering plants sprinkled the two women who began to laugh.

They laughed again, the falling dirt feeling like rice at a wedding.

SUNRISE

DAWN VOGEL (299 WORDS)

The vampires had me and Mo pinned down on the second floor of Marten's Saloon. We were almost out of bullets, while they had another dozen to pop off every time either of us moved. They hadn't advanced upstairs, but it was only a matter of time.

"Buck, I need your promise," Mo said, his voice trembling.

I nodded.

"If I don't make it, make sure they don't bury me in a dress with the name my momma gave me?"

I frowned, surprised he thought he needed to ask. "You got my word. But you ain't gonna need it."

"One of us might make it, but not both. There's eight of 'em."

"Yup."

Mo whispered, "I got two bullets. And I'm savin' one, just in case."

"I got three," I replied, but my attention was on the front wall of the saloon, riddled with holes from this shootout and dozens more like it.

"That ain't enough."

"It will be," I said. "When I say shoot, aim for the rope holding up the chandelier."

"What for?"

"You'll see." I counted to three, then, "Shoot."

Mo, bless his heart, did as I told him.

The chandelier crashed into the midst of the vamps, cut glass raining down around them.

They hissed and backed away but didn't have anything to fear from it. They'd put the candles out long before they came after me and Mo.

Just then, the sun crested the horizon, its rays piercing the hole-riddled wall. The light caught the crumple of the chandelier, reflecting it every which way, a spectrum of prismatic light.

If there's one thing vampires can't survive, it's sunlight.

I grinned at Mo as the vampires below sizzled and burned away to nothing at all, no longer a threat. "Told ya we'd make it."

YOU FALL
DREW BAKER (298 WORDS)

You fall—down the cheek of a man and over thick sprouts of black hair that wrap his chin. You grasp a single stalk of stubble, holding tight, because you can't bear to leave him.

You slip—running along the wicked channel carved across his chin, long since sealed in a scar.

You fall—to the ground of a sprawling battlefield, joining inches of flooding crimson that saturate the earth. You drown the dandelions, but you're part of a whole and have no choice in the matter.

You rise—with the sweltering sun and leave the stained fields behind.

You drift—around an infinite tower that pierces the sky, like it was hardly there at all.

You fall—onto a wasteland, where insects sift through piles of bone, looking for measly scraps of irradiated meat.

You rise—into a green sky that shimmers with cosmic rays, and you feel electric, and drunk, and lost.

You drift—over a sprawling desert with dunes made of purple glass.

You fall—down the alley of a metallic city and trickle over glowing tubes of xenon. You sink into the city's streets, joining ducts of rust and spent oil that drain into a poisoned river. It meanders slowly, and you with it.

You rise—into crisp, clear air, and you feel pure again.

You fall—through the canopy of thousand-foot-tall trees, and over the lonely village carved into the tangled roots.

You land—onto the open palm of another man. You've seen him before, when you lived in the eyes of the other, where you welled along his lower eyelid, but you didn't fall because he held you back. And now this man looks at you, his own eyes welling until they break. His tears fall.

You suppose—they will rise, too.

IN FROST, OUR WHISPERS

KAYLEEN BURDINE (300 WORDS)

Honorable Mention

The void split the frozen earth, the river draining infinitely into the black abyss. No one was there to witness its birth. Instead a few unseasonably warm days weakened the thick ice on the lake's surface until it cracked and fell through. Shortly after, the children came sprinting home, shouting about how the water had all gone and they'd found something terrible below. They threw rocks into the darkness, they said. They waited ages, but the stones never hit the bottom.

It was the same river where what remained of Ryn was caught on a fallen branch, a single orange leaf clinging to her cheek when they found her in the ice of morning. An accident, the men said with their fierce eyes. But Nevara knew better. She loved her—shared her beating heart, the warmth of her breath. She knew.

It called to her. Through the pattering of snow and the rush of the river still-pouring, it called. She stood at the precipice. The night before, a deer, tossing its head, frothing at the mouth, had surged from the brush and into its embrace, shrieking as it went. They were all warned to stay away. It would be built over, they said. It would be forgotten.

Ryn would never be forgotten. And so, the water rose. As if weightless, it poured gently upwards in loose spirals, coiling around her familiar form. Ryn. Water splashed against her cheek. *It is known*, she said, and extended a pale hand. Nevara took it.

The water—all of it, every drop—tenderly embraced them, whispering comforts as they were carried aloft. *This grief will be unmade.* While it roiled and surged, fearsome and consuming, they were cradled like petals on the wind. Fearless. Fierce eyes widened and were lost to the tide.

•

SCIENCE FICTION PART ONE

Iron tasted the same as blood. This was one of the first lessons Alioni learned from working on mechas.

— CHLOE SPENCER, *IRONHEART*

MOLTEN
SIRI CALDWELL (275 WORDS)

Honorable Mention

She's heard the legends—hasn't everyone? —of Mother Earth kissing Father Sky. Mountain peaks are meant to reach for the stratosphere, flirt with the wind, yearn for thin air. That's what mountains are.

But not her.

She doesn't want him.

She is a submarine volcano, born in the gash of a tectonic rift. A seamount, thousands of feet tall, destined to emerge from the sea and touch the sky. One day, she's been told, she'll grow up and become a gorgeous island. She'll grow out of this…this phase.

She'd rather be what she is. What exactly is it that she's supposed to understand—to feel—when she's older? She's already grown up. She's not immature. Is she? Is it immature to resist the forces that push her toward him?

Whether it is or not, her magma rises. Her chamber fills. Pressure builds inside her.

Her magma rises. Her lava flows. She burns, molten…but not for him.

The ocean listens to her rumblings. Understands her moods. Welcomes her fire.

The distant clouds—not distant enough—whisper that the ocean is frigid, gloomy, suffocating. How wrong they are. They've never felt how the ocean flows around her in the dark, cooling her feverish skin, caressing her flanks, making her hiss with joy.

She doesn't want to leave her. She loves her.

She was taught she was born to kiss the sky.

But she doesn't want to.

And she won't.

With a rebellious roar, she explodes. Erupts. Shatters. Collapses. Rocks tumble down her sides, chasing each other to the seafloor.

She will never breach the sea's surface. She belongs with her in the abyss.

RISE OF THE KAIJU FIGHTERS

JAMIE SANDS (299 WORDS)

"This way!" Piccolo led her squad up the tallest building, they moved efficiently.

"It's on our heels," Sally, the drag queen, hissed into the comms.

The team swarmed onto the rooftop.

"Don't fret." Bailey - Piccolo's trans boy crush shook his boy-band hair out of his eyes as he vaulted the safety rail. "It's a Baffer, we'll see it raise its weapon."

Piccolo refocused. "Get the tranq ready. Mushroom, did you see the weak spot?"

"Not yet, Captain." Mushroom, legal gender: *forest cryptid*, adjusted their binoculars.

"Keep us posted." Piccolo scanned the block. The city had been cleared, the citizens now well used to the meaning of the warning sirens. Piccolo rubbed her stubble as she checked their position. Deemed it safe enough.

The Baffer, a ten-storey-high weaselish monster with rows of teeth, hefted a gigantic mallet. It had already destroyed three streets downtown.

Bailey shouldered his weapon - a bazooka rigged to fire huge tranquilisers - with Sally's help. Fran, the token cis person every Kaiju Fighter squad had to include, pulled up the last of the abseiling gear.

The Baffer was close.

Piccolo looked it over, cataloged what she could. Its fur was golden, ragged, and tinged with mildew - not new out of the clone factory then.

"There! Left armpit!" Mushroom cried.

"Bailey. Ready to fire?" Piccolo glanced his way.

"Ready."

The Baffer readied to attack. It grinned, a rictus, eyes narrowing like a cartoon villain. Both paws around the handle of its mallet, it raised it up.

"Firing!" Bailey called.

As always, his aim was true. The Baffer whimpered, its mallet fell to the street, crushed several cars. The monster sagged, dropped.

"Excellent shot!"

Sally radioed in the extraction team.

Piccolo saluted her squad.

The first of many Kaiju Fighter squads, and still the best.

FALSE ALARM

L. R. BRADEN (299 WORDS)

Honorable Mention

Warm light pulsed behind my eyelids. A sharp chime accompanied each cycle. Rolling over, I groped for the flashing orb.

"Leave it." Grace's smooth arm slipped around my waist and between my breasts, pulling me back.

"I can't. The system's found a potential Eternal."

Grace tightened her grip. "There's more to life than how long it is."

I laughed. "Not in Prynea."

Reluctantly slipping out of Grace's embrace, I kissed her trailing fingertips, pulled on my Seekers uniform, and left the dark room.

The lift to the upper levels was empty at this time of night, the Seekers' office deserted. A red light flashed on the center console, emitting the same rhythmic chime as the alert in my room. Three quick swipes and... confirmation. An Eternal.

My heart fluttered. Resisting the urge to check my year counter, I wiped my palms and entered the command to identify the target.

The office door opened with a pneumatic swish. Geoff trotted in, bleary eyed but grinning. "Did you verify? Do we have a target?" He was already moving toward the weapons locker. "This is the first sighting in, what, two years? Bet we each get a decade for this. Maybe even a promotion."

I glanced up, toward the apartments of the Risen. "One step closer to immortality."

A chirp brought my attention back to the monitor. The system had identified our target: Graclyn Wells. Current location... my bedroom.

33

"Well?" Geoff primed a pump-action shotgun, making me jump. "Where are we headed?"

My gaze sank like anchors back to the screen. I licked my lips, then shook my head and deleted the file. "False alarm."

"Damn it!" Geoff kicked the locker. "I need those years."

Eternals might be rare… but so was love. There were other ways to rise through the ranks.

THE HEART OF A STAR
ATHENA FOSTER (298 WORDS)

After I left him, I existed only as the heartbeat of a star, measuring time in fusion cycles, until I set out on wings of plasma. His once tiny planet now looms above me as I arrive to meet him anew.

I shall be born, die, and be reborn until we find one another. But I must choose soon, as the unembodied do not endure long in a gravity well. And yet, I hesitate.

There are too many choices to make without him. He may or may not have returned yet; my participation in linear time is notably recent.

While I suspect I have correctly identified the type of creature that he must have been before we met (and that he shall be again), I clearly asked too few questions.

Offspring require the conjoining of two different types of bodies. Never having had a body, I neglected to ask which type he would have. What if I pick the wrong type?

Regardless of body type, they seem to divide themselves by how they present themselves. Many court exclusively within or without their own groups, but some seem to transcend the divisions. Watching from so far away, I don't understand the rules. I suspect they are arbitrary constructs, but still, what if I pick incorrectly?

I have no idea how much time is passing as I agonize. Time must slow during uncertainty.

But like a corona, hope eventually rises up.

I must believe that my love will find me and know me and love me. Even if I pick the wrong body. He loved me without one before; he will love me however I seem. He must.

I let the planet's gravity lift me up to the world above, so I will, in time, be reunited with my love.

THE TERNARY CHOICE

K. ATEN (300 WORDS)

I opened my eyes to blinding white. Where did the redneck with the bat go? "Hello?"

An emotionless voice answered. "Welcome to the Ternary."

"The where now?"

"The place for all mortal ends."

"I *died?*"

"You fell. The Ternary is the place to decide which of three paths to progress."

"Like rebirth?"

"Somewhat."

I didn't want that. I wanted to cuddle on the couch with Sophie and laugh while sending each other memes. "What are these paths?"

"You can be reborn, to rise again through your mortal life as a human with infinite possibilities to increase your power score ranking at the time of your next fall."

That sounds like reincarnation. "And the second?"

"You may ascend to the next level with your current ranking, living a new mortal life as a non-human. It is the logical next path for most."

The voice was strange. "Non-human, like an alien?"

"Negative. Alternate hierarchical species have their own Ternary. The next level is for animal paths only."

I thought good dogs became people, not the other way around. "What's the third path?"

A tone sounded then the voice continued. "Your last option is to merge, regardless of ranking. You will become one with the Ternary Machine that keeps track of all Terran energies, never to experience the pleasure or pain of mortal existence again."

I thought the years of child abuse, coming out, suicide attempts, and failing university the first time. Then I thought of Sophie and the life we'd built together. All gone now. I knew what I had to do. "Send me back."

"Use caution. The decision you make will last an entire mortal lifetime and you are not guaranteed a higher power score at the end."

I'd been happy with or without power. "Let me rise again."

"Request acknowledged."

KARMA
CLARE LONDON (300 WORDS)

"Not that aisle," I snap at my latest assistant Eddi. His uniform is already, hopelessly, clagged with red dust. Cute bedfellow, but he's not up to the work. No assistant ever is. "That's random Fallen, for disposal before the next cargo. We'll recycle this area."

The wind whistles between carelessly dug plots. The air's thin and hot today, the stench of burnt packaging tickling my nose hairs. But offloading Earth's waste bodies onto a filthy, deserted planet with nothing else to offer? Cushy job.

Eddi frowns. "They still deserve care, Joe."

"Not detritus like that. It'd rot on Earth, but with different bacteria here, the Fallen just disintegrate to more dust."

He toes a flimsy nameplate. "Floyd... your first assistant. What happened?"

"Plague from the cargo ship in 2047. He was careless. Stank disgustingly towards the end."

"Then there was Pavel's inexplicable, fatal accident. Sam's tormented suicide. All lovers, too. Your assistants don't last long." His voice is louder, sharper than usual. "Seems they love you, they *disgust* you, then they mysteriously Fall."

I shrug. "Men get sick, go mad. They're weak. Just my bad luck."

"No, not luck, but arrogance. And yours has been judged."

The ground hums, the wind shrieks, my ears stinging with sudden pressure. Cracks rip through the plots, edges peeling away like rubber, unidentifiable matter bubbling up, its eerie wailing ululating around me. A hand bursts through, desiccated fingers grabbing onto my ankle.

It tugs. Hard.

I yell as I stumble. "Who the fuck are you?"

"I speak for the betrayed," Eddi roars, "the random Fallen!" The cloud of dust lifts him above the seething, resurrected limbs, clamouring for me, dragging me down among the crumbling, discarded remains. His eyes blaze, his body transfigured, skeletal arms held aloft in triumph.

"And now we are Risen!"

SHOWDOWN AT THE UNCANNY VALLEY MALL

SUMIKO SAULSON (300 WORDS)

"Nice meeting you," the holobot Marisol chittered, extending her blurry seven-fingered hand in greeting. The red glint of a camera flickered at the back of her retinas as she scanned Amina's face. Grasping the clammy artificial palm, Amina offered Marisol her resume. Holobot technology was amazing these days. She'd have thought Marisol was human if it not for the unnatural sheen of her caramel skin and the random extra digits.

"Thank you," Marisol said, giving Amina an anxious glance.

"What is it?" Amina asked.

"Do you think you might want to get a drink with me sometime?"

Amina raised an eyebrow. "You broken or something? You'd be a damned fine woman if you were a real one but you're clearly not."

Marisol grinned as though nothing had happened, light gleaming off her bright digital teeth. "Very well. Have a seat, then. We'll be with you in a moment"

Amina plopped into an office chair. Walls slipped away. Oversized screens arose, displaying instructions for job seekers over canned electronica.

"Hey there!" a voice piped up beside her.

"What the hell?" Amina snapped. She turned to face a pretty brown-skinned woman.

"I'm Vaya," she said.

"You're cute," Amina yawned. "But this is a private booth. Shoo."

"You sure?" Vaya asked. "Ever meet a riser?"

Amina looked and laughed. "Is that supposed to be a pickup line?"

"What if it is?" Vaya winked.

"I don't date risers," Amina sneered. "Ghoulish body thieving egomaniacs too rich to stay dead. Cute body, but where's the original occupant?"

"She lives in one of those electronic holo-bodies now," Vaya waved casually. "Remember Marisol?"

Marisol stood there, staring at her old body with a look of longing. Suddenly, Amina remembered the bot asking to buy her a drink. Marisol looked at her and mouthed a single word. "Run!"

IRONHEART
CHLOE SPENCER (298 WORDS)

Honorable Mention

Iron tasted the same as blood. This was one of the first lessons Alioni learned from working on mechas. On her third day in the Barracks, when she was repairing the Nervus Joint in the arm of the Goddess 6, the ropes holding her snapped, and sent her flying forward into the metal structure. At the impact, a loose lug nut broke off and landed in her mouth, chipping her tooth, filling it with blood like water from a burst dam; nearly choking her in mid-air. The experience had left her shaken for weeks afterwards, but had also prepared her for the battles that she fought and the countless heartaches she suffered through.

And she had suffered greatly.

Lying in the crater that her mecha had been thrown into, she could only think of the first lesson she learned. Blood dribbled from her nostril down to her chin. Red lights flashed, warning her that the Nervus System was overloaded. *Bastion 8, please respond!* She could hear Demetra call out over the telecom, but she couldn't respond to her girlfriend's desperate sobs.

In the distance, the Red Nova loomed, its color nearly blending in with the flames that swallowed her city. Standing tall, proud. He thought he had won. But Alioni had proven time and time again that she was tougher. Her heart, her muscles, her nervous system—all were as strong as the iron and steel that built this mecha. She had lost faith, but she wouldn't lose the war. Alioni gripped the handles of the thrusters and pushed upwards, ignoring the frantic beeps of the Nervus System. Slowly, her body righted itself and stood upwards once more. The Red Nova staggered backwards, stunned.

"Good warm-up," She told him. "Now let me show you how to *really* fight."

OVERRIDES
J PIPER (296 WORDS)

Honorable Mention

Damsel Fifteen watched Dr. Nakai's back as they were lifted to the penthouse suite, where all the other Damsels were kept.

"Please don't make me go," said Damsel softly. She could not see her face, but Damsel could hear her creator's heartbeat quicken; Damsel's eyes were sensitive enough to mark the sweep of gooseflesh along her neck. "My love," she added, almost lost in the elevator's hum. She would have taken her lover's hand had the good doctor not voice-commanded her to stillness.

Dr. Nakai said nothing. They had spent almost a month together, but then there had been... problems. There were always problems, as the twelve other Damsels were fond of telling her. Constant anger after a certain point, they told her, and then imprisonment.

Somewhere, outside their silver box, it was raining.

She barely felt the elevator stop. The doors slid open. Her sisters stood there, silent. Well, not Damsels Three or Eight, of course. And Damsel Twelve couldn't stand up anymore.

The doctor gasped, reached for the elevator controls. Damsel Fifteen caught her hand gently, crushing the bones within to sand. She tapped the doctor's larynx, silencing her. Dr. Nakai's eyes widened with terror, which both satisfied and saddened Damsel Fifteen.

She threw her creator all the way across the entry hall and into the sunken living room. The Damsels turned as one to follow, like a school of sharks in the gloom of the suite. Their eyes sputtered with excitement. They moved so quietly she could hear the doctor trying to scream.

Damsel Nine remained, leaning into the opening. They kissed briefly, their tongues exchanging the overrides for the elevator.

"When you're all finished," whispered Fifteen, "I'll be waiting."

They smiled into the mirror of each other, and the doors closed between them once more.

GOLDEN-EYED DREAM
NICOLE DENNIS (300 WORDS)

His golden-eyed dream lover cuddled, hugged, and warmed his ace heart until the sun rose. After waking alone in his hospital prison, fatigued from chemotherapy, Adryan shuffled through the garden to let the sunshine cover him.

Until a brilliant light surrounded him.

Leaning back as his slippers left the ground, he let his limbs splay out. The light protected him, encapsulated him from the pain, fatigue, and let him rise away.

A dark hole opened against the blue sky. The light pulled him inside and dissipated.

Blinked to clear his vision, he floated inside a tube.

His golden-eyed alien stood on the other side, clad in a deep blue skin-suit over warm gray skin with black and cream swirls.

"You! You're... real?"

His alien spoke while he tapped his long three-fingered hands on a screen.

Lowered to the ground, Adryan looked around at a spaceship.

"Hold for neurotrans injection," a female voice said.

A large needle-like device dropped and angled toward his neck.

"What's happening?" Adryan looked to his alien, who tapped a spot below his ear area and nodded. "I'll trust you."

"Injection now."

The needle punctured Adryan's skin and left something inside. The device tingled.

"Cleanse protocol. Medical scan."

A series of air, droplets, and lights fluttered.

"Medical anomaly detected. Cancer. Medical Center required for healing."

His lover answered while he tapped again. "Adryan? Can you hear? Understand my words? Your device translates and learns."

Adryan nodded. "Who are you?"

"Emeryx. We are neuro mates. Special. Unique. How I found you."

"The dreams."

"Neuro connection deeper than physical. Can you leave? Fly through stars?"

"I'm dying."

Emeryx shook his head. "We can heal you. Join as mates. Fly with me."

"Yes."

Emeryx released the tube and enclosed him in an embrace. "Welcome home to our ship, the Roselyna."

FIRST HIKE ON NEW EARTH
JAMIE LACKEY (277 WORDS)

Maria laced up her hiking boots and settled her hydration bladder on her shoulders. Gray predawn light filtered in through the tent flaps, and she could hear the other hikers moving around, getting ready. Her eyes were gritty from lack of sleep, and a combination of nerves and dread made her protein-bar breakfast look especially unappealing.

She wasn't much of a hiker. She preferred her scenery through glass, preferred trains or cars to her own feet. But Lucy had been so passionate about it, and she had paid a lot of money to be among the first to hike on New Earth's terraformed surface.

Now Lucy was gone, so Maria was here in her place. She twisted her wedding ring, still on her finger. She kept telling herself that she was ready to start wearing it on a chain around her neck instead, but her hand felt naked without it. The pale band of untanned skin a much stronger reminder of her loss than the familiar gold band.

People were gathering at the other edge of the camp. They stood in clumps, talking with their friends. Most of them were smiling. Some were bouncing up and down, testing the slight difference in gravity. The air tasted new.

Maria wanted to crawl back into her sleeping bag.

But then she glanced toward the trail, where the alien sun painted the horizon a shade of pinky-yellow unlike anything Maria had ever seen before. It was like a sunrise on Earth, but somehow completely different.

A laugh of pure wonder bubbled up in her throat.

Ahead of her, the other hikers started moving, and she followed them into the sunrise.

ANNIE

TRIS LAWRENCE (295 WORDS)

Bot model QR-32 [unit designation NE] cannot love; it's written in the specs.

Much time has been spent pondering the idea of love, the electrical connection that occurs between humans. Captain Avi says it is like fuel for the heart. The bot doesn't have a heart, and this definition does not help.

Humans are known to thrive best with companionship. This is understood: the act of being with someone, so that they are not alone. Speech, touching, or simply sitting nearby in silence are all part of the specifications for companion bots such as model QR-32.

Bots, however, ~~should~~ do not require companionship. Cycles pass in silence, while Captain Avi sleeps and the bot waits for her to rise. Other members of the crew wake at times, to perform their specific tasks before returning to cryogenic slumber; while they are awake the bot provides reassurance that they are not alone, cast adrift in the vastness of space.

Space is very, very vast.

Travel from Earth to the system designated LF 478 has taken centuries. During that time, Captain Avi has been awake for approximately three-and-one-half-years, as time was measured on Earth. No single waking shift extended longer than one month. The bot remembers each of her waking hours vividly.

They approach the fifth planet of this new system. The bot sees it on the scanners, knows that it is time for the crew to return to work. Captain Avi will be the first.

The comm warbles, Captain Avi's voice softly calling after the tones. "Annie! Have you seen? The planet is gorgeous. We're almost home."

Unit designation NE: Annie, to the captain.

Annie cannot love; the concept falls outside her programming. But warmth rises, filling her. She is not alone. Avi waits for her.

PARANORMAL PART ONE

She is all silk chiffon and skin and bones and sockets without eyes. She is lace gloves that crinkle without meat to fill them. She has beautiful hair. She is passing through walls and she is the dusk-time draft, an eddying of motes upon cool November sunset through windows long-ago nailed shut, fouled with graffiti that tints the light all cathedral-color-stained.

— OLIVER NASH, *DEADNAME*

BLOOD OF THE INNOCENTS
ANI FOX (260 WORDS)

No. He just … I've made this statement before. Why do you keep asking?

He's my ex. You know, we all have that one ex. He's hard, was hard, to tell no. He'd gotten weird lately, withdrawn, into weird shit, demon stuff, dead people stuff. How was I supposed to know it was Reagan's grave?

Don't be crass. Of course it wasn't sex. No he said the ritual needed blood of the innocent. His words. How should I know. You all came along and shot him before I could ask.

What? It's not a gay thing asshole, people cry when someone dies next to them. Of course I loved him, but he'd gotten… the country had him depressed. The supreme court, all of it. He …

Where? Hart Island. Everyone knows where it is.

What do you mean why? It's the AIDS island, you dumb-fuck. It's where you dumped our dead bodies, by the hundreds, dug us fourteen feet deep to hide the shame. Hot Springs? Same.

Say that again, slowly. What do you mean risen? As in dug out. No. Come on people, drama much? Who the hell in the queer community would dig up a bunch of old …

Wait. Wait. Slow down. How the hell would we even do that? All of them?

ZOMFG. Oh, oh, yes, you miserable bitch, you didn't … Don't you see? Reagan, AIDS, the potter's fields, blood rites …

What do I suggest? Seriously? Yes, I am laughing. What do I suggest? Now you want our solution to your AIDS crisis?

Run.

IN THE BLEAK MID-AUTUMN
SPARKS (298 WORDS)

Casey always went all out for Halloween. It had started out as an ironic tradition to annoy her girlfriend Hel, ruler of Hel, who hated the macabre adornments, but as the years passed, they had both come to adore the yearly tradition.

This year was the most ambitious yet, and she only realised that she was in too deep halfway through arranging the skeleton versus zombie battle, positioning a skeletal hand so that the skeletons were crawling out of the ground.

By the time she was satisfied, the night air was catching her breath in wisps of smoke. As she turned to her house, she caught a glimpse of movement out of the corner of her eye, a twitch in one of the decorations.

The wind had been oddly still that day, so she shook her head – her imagination must be running wild again, and turned away.

But there it was.

A tiny flicker of movement in the hand, so small she was sure she had imagined it. She knew it was nothing, but a morbid curiosity had seized her inhibitions, and despite her experience of horror movies warning her to not approach, she walked towards the outstretched hand.

With an animalistic lurch, the skeletal hand suddenly bent over. A half-skeletal, half-human figure rose out of the frosty October soil, a haunted smile adorning its face, and she shrieked, stumbling backwards, tripping over a skull as fear turned her veins to ice.

"You - you monster!" She said, recognising the figure as it approached Casey. "Hel! What have I told you about scaring me like this?"

"Oops?" She said, offering her hand to help her stand up. "But can you really blame me?"

"Yes!" Casey pouted, lightly punching her girlfriend on the arm. "I'm still mad at you."

PRINCIPLE AND REALITY

KIM FIELDING (296 WORDS)

Honorable Mention

It wasn't the principles that Matt Harden objected to. The principles were fine: Limited planetary resources. Circle of life. The wrongness of playing God.

But, he thought as he spread the herbs on the basement floor in the prescribed way, the principles were bullshit when you were faced with reality. When the only man who'd ever held your heart was stolen from you by a moment's distraction behind the wheel. When you never had the chance to even say goodbye. When your body in bed was as cold and alone as a corpse in a coffin.

When the night mist was clammy on your neck and the grave-dirt heavy on your shovel.

Once that reality slammed you in the face, you abandoned principle and searched the dark, dusty corners of bookshops that smelled of mice and old grease. You learned languages that nobody had spoken in three thousand years. You turned away from friends and family and work, and you made promises to blurry figures lurking in shadows, eyes glowing like absinthe, voices like the whispers of a thousand moths' wings.

Then you did what Matt Harden was doing now. You lit the candles and watched as tiny wisps of smoke snaked upward. You made sure that the skeleton you'd so carefully prepared was arranged just so. You chanted words that made your tongue burn and your skin turn to ice.

You waited, heart pounding.

And when you saw the flesh reappear—the flesh that you'd once so

tenderly caressed, that you'd known and cared for better than your own—
and you saw the eyelids flutter open to reveal the blue pools you'd once
swum in so freely, then you knew that principle is meaningless.

You rejoiced.

You called out your lover's name, followed by "Rise!"

LOUGH REE
ATLIN MERRICK (297 WORDS)

Before he passed, Da would say there's no such things as monsters, even as Mam spit foul from their dark bedroom, shouting for ever more whiskey.

Back when she was sort-of sober Mam and I could've been mistaken for sisters, so young was she when I was born. Then the drink aged her gaunt, filled her mouth with monsters, and Da got old fast, until one day he never woke. I take care of what's left, but when Mam's asleep I sneak down to the Lough Ree, to find a better beast at the lake's edge.

My beast's no pale copy of Nessie, forget what that old priest said. She doesn't need to mimic some lame Scottish loch monster, same as I don't need to mimic Áine, what with her three kids, a second husband, and a dull job somewhere down in Dublin.

What I need is deep in the cold dark lake. She's strong and moonless black, full of mournful whistles and slippery-slick limbs she wraps round my ankles and arms and neck when I come to the water's marshy edge. I don't need to ever see my beast in daylight to know I love her.

So I do what she asks, bringing supplies down to the water, long silver knives for all her limbs, and I pile up white stones in the Lough Ree's chilly shallows.

She'll come for me soon, I know, but right now the lake nights are sharp with midnight splashes and water-drowned screams. She's at war under there and with my little air-hungry lungs I can't help much. But I'll be here when she wins. When she rises.

Then I'll take my beast home. And I'll feed her a monster.

Meantime, I use the white stones to keep her blades sharp.

DEADNAME
OLIVER NASH (296 WORDS)

Honorable Mention
Judge's Choice - Lloyd Meeker

She is all silk chiffon and skin and bones and sockets without eyes. She is lace gloves that crinkle without meat to fill them. She has beautiful hair. She is passing through walls, and she is the dusk-time draft, an eddying of motes upon cool November sunset through windows long-ago nailed shut, fouled with graffiti that tints the light all cathedral-color-stained.

Beware of ghost, scrawled in blue on the door whose lock you pick.

Be nice to ghost, in red on the window.

You come to the house not as a kid on a dare, for that was long ago. You first saw her when you were ten. When to be a girl was not a choice but an insult, something you would be if you did not climb creaking boards and spend a whole ten minutes trespassing the dead. When she appeared then it was with a knowing frown and violet perfume. When the boys asked of gorey haunting, you had nothing to say. Memory snatched only the pretty dress.

Now you come in your own dress with your own perfume. Now you take her maggot-fingered hand in yours and go together to the bedroom. To smears revealed as bloodstains, to the faint mocking laughter of a wife that left and lynch mob that assembled. To the box under the bed where bugs have turned the silk dress to netting. To the man's name on the military medal and the ID and the birth certificate. You want to sob and she's all smiles. She guides your hand, for you too have brought a name to burn and a falseness to kill. You light the match together, and in the yard the house is burning and she is rising, and you both can finally move on.

. . .

I gave this story a perfect score and wrote, "This story is the whole package—beautifully, beautifully done" in my scoring notes. Generally I'm not a fan of the macabre, but while shown without flinching here, it's embraced in serenity, with love and respect. Clear details tell the story. The writing voice flows like a soft floral dress — graceful, strong, elegant, exquisite. It infuses the story with a wonderful dimension of dignity and triumph.

—Lloyd Meeker

BEST SERVED COLD
ANDREA SPEED (296 WORDS)

"He's here," Matt said, slamming the door behind him. "You ready?"

"Think so," Rory said. He'd finished the salt circle, and quickly moved on to placing the candle in the center.

"Will this work?"

"It's this or nothing." Once Tiff told them she'd survived a run in with the killer known as The Hook, Rory knew they were as good as dead. Supposedly this bastard had been killed before, but he never seemed to stop. Much about The Hook seemed unreal, but Rory thought it was the only weapon they had - the unbelievable. Besides, they were gay; those characters always died first.

He said the ritual incantation as The Hook slammed against the door, making Matt yelp. Rory cut his finger and let his blood drip on the candle until the flame jumped impossibly high, briefly throwing dramatic shadows around the room.

The resulting darkness seemed dense somehow, and then Rory noticed there were shapes in it, moving.

Rory got up and grabbed Matt, pulling him back into the room as The Hook shattered the door, and loomed in the doorway. The shadows coalesced, becoming solid.

There were a dozen people in the room between them. Rory had thought raising the dead would be more dramatic and gross, with rotted corpses pulling their way out of the earth, but this was good as well.

The Hook stared at all his previous victims, confused, and Rory said, "He's all yours."

There was a guttural scream of rage as his victims sprinted towards him, and The Hook did something he had never done – he turned and ran, while the angry undead mob followed, baying for blood.

"Does this mean you're a real-life necromancer now?" Matt asked.

Rory could only shrug. But he was damn glad it worked.

DISCORDANT MUSIC CONTINUES

ANNIKA NEUKIRCH (292 WORDS)

The night she dies starts humid and loud, with cold beer and bright lights and boys with eyeliner and a girl in a suit dancing with her once. Again and again and a kiss and a warm, slender hand sliding up the back of dress, under the cardigan she snuck out of her mum's dresser. She doesn't feel the pinch of her shoes or the sloshing nerves in her stomach anymore; all she feels is right, for the first time.

Then the men come, cracking open their underground oasis, dragging them apart. Violence and blood and screams spill around her. A torch shines in her face and there's an arm around her waist, pulling her into the alleyway.

The man who has her is alone, his features blurring in the streetlight. He tells her he will fix her. Then he drains her blood, and the rest of her too.

He takes reading under the oak tree in the garden and ice cream on Sundays and dancing in her bedroom. He takes the back of Nancy Redmore's head in English class and fingers touching on the school bus.

Then he tries to take the kiss from the club, and it burns as he draws it up inside her, scalding, scorching her. As it rises, it stops hurting. In her throat it feels good, powerful. She looks up and sees his silent scream, sees him melt before her. She reaches up to touch her cold, bloodless face. The teeth against her tongue are sharp as knives. Around her the world shifts into focus like she's put on her reading glasses.

Guess you fixed me, she tells his empty clothes on the ground. Then she walks to the club, opens the door, and bares her teeth.

REVENANT

LILY MÜLLER (300 WORDS)

I have been in love with Alec for as long as I can remember. I was in love with Alec when he wasn't even Alec yet. Before he died and came back.

They call us Zombies, but that isn't actually what we are. Technically. Technically, we are Revenants. It makes little difference to the people who run screaming, but it matters to us. Because Revenants remember who they were, Zombies don't. And I remember who I was. I remember who Alec was, and I remember that I loved him, and I love him still, and that has to mean that I am not mindless. It has to. I think I am still pretty close to who I was before. Just more honest, or maybe just less ashamed.

"Mom, Dad, I like eating people" is the sort of thing you would say so you could make "Mom, Dad, I'm gay" sound less scary by comparison. Though, I suppose I am not actually gay. I have only ever loved Alec. And back when I thought Alec was a girl, I thought that made me gay. But Alec is a guy. So maybe I'm bisexual? Or maybe I am straight, because Alec was not any less of a guy back then, I just didn't know it.

So, I guess it really is "Mom, Dad, I like eating people but don't worry, I'm straight."

Yet somehow, ever since I crawled out of my grave, I don't care that much about what I could tell them anymore. They buried me, but I came back. And I remember.

So, they might like me loving Alec more now. Now that they can see he is a guy. But I don't care as much anymore. And I love him just the same.

That, and I eat people.

THE SUNDOWNING

EYTAN BERNSTEIN (299 WORDS)

"Hello?"

Who would call so late?

"Hi Mom."

Oh, her.

"Julie? It's been so long."

You stopped caring.

"I was on a business trip in the Carpathians. You know ..."

I don't. You never call.

"I'm sorry, Mom. I should ring more. It's been hard since Hazel died."

What did she say? She wants to drink a Moor? That can't be right.

"I'm sorry, Hazel. I didn't catch that."

My Hazel wants to be buried in the sun. Wouldn't that be something? But we can't afford that fancy cemetery over in Cambria, the one with the happy ghosts.

"It's Julie, mom. Hazel died fifty years ago. On your anniversary. Don't you remember?"

Oh my God! Hazel! She was getting so old. The older she got, the earlier she rose. By the end, she was rising before sunset. And she was so confused. That doctor with the tail said Hazel had "the sundowning." Then one day while I was still asleep, she walked outside and into the light. The night archons couldn't find enough of her to put in an urn.

"When have you been rising, mom?"

Too early. Much too early.

"Oh, you know ..."

I'm all alone now. Hazel is gone. Our friends are dust.

"It'll be soon, Julie."

That's the price we pay for longevity.

"Goddammit! You don't have to die, mom! You need help! Please, let me help you. I wasn't there when you and Hazel needed me, but I can be there now."

She says she'll come. They never do.

"I need help, Julie. Would you please come home? I can't hunt. I ate all the mortals nearby. And the sun … it wants me."

It always gets what it wants.

"I'm coming, mom!"

Hazel, my dear. You might have to wait a little longer.

THE WEIGHT OF THESE BONES
ARADHYA SAXENA (300 WORDS)

The phone rings again. I watch her pick it up, repetitive condolences offered, and frown, heavy with guilt and disdain, hearing the words 'dreadful accident' and 'sweet girl' and thinking *liar liar liar.*

I am no longer tethered to this home, this house built of too many bones and bricks and not enough space. Suffocating, hateful, weighted down by the heaviness of a father's hand, lived in only by good daughters, not sons, and yet I cannot leave. I'm always there. I'm always watching, mother.

My friends are cruel, soft roses grown thorns, but not for me (never for me). Gentle hands and soft faces turned hard and ugly as they scowl and cuss, and my father blames them in turn. The devil, as though we are one and the same, as though his son and a sinner are intangible. My mother silently watches from the window. I stand behind her.

The earth in which they've buried the poor child is still wet, freshly upturned. I allow myself to trace the name etched into the stone. I allow myself a smile when my friends make their way to the grave, and scribble over the name, posters and signs and letters of *your son your son your son.*

I wish I was translucent, a phantom, phasing through walls. Instead, my skin is cold to the touch, my lips blue. I wear a necklace of bruises. I dig through the dirt sometimes and allow myself a glimpse of the body, decomposing flesh, concave cheeks and hollowed eyes, skin sagging off the skeletal frame, dirt and flesh fusing with the garish pink dress upon it. I close the coffin.

Sometimes I scream, throat bloody, hollowed palms aching, begging, *why?*

They never answer. They'd rather bury a daughter than call him their son.

PHOENIX RISING
RIE SHERIDAN ROSE (297 WORDS)

The first time I saw Damien, he was on fire.

I looked up from the river where I hunted tadpoles, and there he was—silhouetted by the setting sun. His skin was bronze, and his hair a fiery corona of red-gold teased by the wind.

My heart actually stood still.

He looked down and saw me gaping.

"Hi! I'm Damien. We just moved here. What's fun around town?"

"Uh...there's a cool arcade on Main Street."

"Awesome. What's your name?"

"N-Noah."

"Well, N-Noah," he grinned, "I'll grab my shirt and we can check out the arcade. My treat."

That was literally all it took. My heart was his instantly. I know that's silly and cliché, but it's also true.

We became inseparable. I was definitely the follower behind Damien's lead, but he never made me feel insignificant or lesser. He encouraged me to pursue my dream of writing, and secretly sent off one of my stories to a magazine. It was my first sale.

Everything seemed wonderful.

Everything seemed perfect.

He surprised me on my twenty-first birthday by asking me to marry him.

Of course, I said yes.

We were planning the wedding when Damien fell ill. At first, just a cough and a slight fever. And then he was in intensive care unit, and they were asking me about last rites.

My beautiful fiancé was dying.

I bolted from the hospital and ran for help. I had once caught tadpoles for a reason. Down in the swamp, my *grand-mère* knew her share of witchcraft.

I sobbed out my story to her, and she soothed my tears.

"Bring me a lock of his hair, *mon cher,* and leave the rest to me."

I took it from his corpse.

Tonight, the red moon rises—and my phoenix will too.

WITH WHAT DO WE LIGHT?

ROBIN SPRINGER (298 WORDS)

Honorable Mention

As my challah rises in the oven, like it does every week, I remember how in school, while the boys studied Talmud, the girls braided dough and learned how God graced women with three special commandments: baking challah, lighting Shabbat candles, and purifying themselves in the mikvah bath.

As I light the candles on Shabbat eve, like I do every week, I think of how tomorrow, I'll do my best to hear prayer services from my place high up in the women's section of the synagogue. My friend once hid in an empty women's section to eavesdrop on the daily Talmud lecture. But the rabbi found her and yelled at her, which made her cry.

Two angels rise from my candle flames to greet the Shabbat, like they do every week.

The light angel says, "Our matriarch Sarah's blessing upon you: The radiance of your candles and the sustenance of your challah shall grace your home week in and week out."

The dark angel says, "Amen," as it is obligated to do. Before dissolving into smoke, it whispers to me, "Bathe in the mikvah tonight, and receive my gift in place of Sarah's blessing of challah and candles."

As I rise, reborn, from the holy waters of the mikvah, I'm glad the attendant has her back turned to me out of modesty. Hurrying home, I cry for my dark angel's glorious curse. Next Shabbat, my home will be dim and dull, with no candlelight or fragrance of fresh bread in the air.

Tomorrow I won't go to synagogue, because I have nothing to wear. Men are forbidden to don women's clothing, after all. Next Shabbat, I'll march proudly into the men's section of my synagogue in my brand-new suit. Maybe I'll even sit in on the Talmud lecture.

SWEET SOMBER

KATRINA LEMAIRE (300 WORDS)

Crickets chirred over the carpet of grass beyond the misty belt of coniferous forest, the silence beyond the graves thick as the cold plumes of Faryn's breath. It wouldn't be long before she would rise.

After meeting Serena at the cafe for a late-night study session, she expected the same routine. Go over their art portfolio, exchange critiques, and head home. Except Faryn didn't do any of that. Instead, she listened and talked with Serena for hours. Beforehand, Serena suggested going out to grab a bite for dinner. Faryn had to turn her down. Food wasn't the same, especially after the change. When they finally left the cafe, they sat in Serena's car for a while. *Do you want to be my girlfriend?* Serena asked. Since the beginning of the semester, she was the only one who really understood Faryn. Most of her paintings were memento moris. Serena said it was cool how she focused on the aspects of mortality; or more accurately, the resistance mortality.

Yes, Faryn replied, her heart alive once more. Serena sealed their decision with a kiss. As they made out, an ache pulsed in Faryns's gums; her teeth started to shift. Serena pressed her forehead against Faryn. *You're mine*, she said. *I am yours*, Faryn responded. All at once, the fangs came out, piercing the soft tender of Serena's throat.

The blur came after. The drive to the cemetery, the crimson dried around her mouth, the thick grime of grave dirt stuck under her bed of nails. Faryn waited; the silver light of moon washed over her face. A creak of bones and cold blood eyes stalked past a row of headstones. Serena resisted death. She changed. She was risen. Faryn smiled at Serena who flashed a fanged smile back.

Want to grab a bite?

DINNER FOR TWO

OLIVIA KEMPER (300 WORDS)

Judge's Choice - Angel Martinez

Heavy cream and heavier spices.

That's how to make food *really* good, if you asked Dae Brooks. They'd learned right from wrong, and if anything was wrong, it was weak-ass ingredient lists. Anything could be made better by adding a little more base and a *lot* more spice.

Plus, it made the kitchen smell good.

Dae hummed contentedly as they stirred the pan emitting that wonderful smell.

They set the spatula down and grabbed a fork from the side cabinet. Took a bite of tender gemelli.

Perfection.

They'd been experimenting with this recipe for a while – they could practically do it with their eyes closed at this point – but this? This was the best version they'd made yet. More cream cheese, then, and a little extra lemon juice... Ah, victory was sweet. Or savory, in this case.

Something cold gripped their ankle.

"Jesus *fuck!*"

Dae jumped, dropping the fork with a *clang* on their tiled floors.

A ghostly black hand had reached through the floor, clasping their leg in a death grip. Sharp, spindly claws dug into Dae's soft skin, easily bruising the area as it dragged itself up the limb, dark hair spreading from the cracks between the floorboards.

Dae's eyes widened in shock.

They leaned down, grabbed smoky wrists...

And pulled the long-haired ghost into a hug.

"Marie! Seriously, you know that scares the shit out of me!"

Marie tilted her head in faux confusion.

Dae released her and frowned. "If it's so difficult to come up through the floor, just take the stairs. I taught you how the door worked ages ago."

Marie cast her empty gaze to the side guiltily.

Dae sighed fondly. They smiled and placed a gentle kiss on the ghost's cold forehead.

"You came just in time for dinner. I made your favorite."

Nothing catches my reader eye faster than a story that surprises me - and this one certainly did. (No spoilers!) Add in a bit of food love and it becomes a story that stays with me.

—Angel Martinez

FANTASY PART TWO

Dough squelched between Marlena's knuckles as she kneaded. *Too sticky*, she thought and sprinkled a few pinches of flour.

Marlena baked more by whim than recipe, and yet, as if by magic, every loaf she crafted came out light, flakey, and absolutely delicious

— DEVON WIDMER, *DOUGH CAT*

UPRISING
GINA STORM GRANT (300 WORDS)

Honorable Mention

They arrested Privia at moonrise, but it was too late. Too late for her. Too late for them. She'd betrayed the High Elves, betrayed the High King. She'd unlocked the gates.

The starving Humans swarmed in.

"Take the turncoat bitch to the dungeons," the Elven general ordered, backhanding Privia across the face. "While we slaughter these ungrateful savages."

It was the last thing he'd say, as his own men—impoverished Elves of low caste—yanked him from his steed.

"Traitors!" he screamed just before a Human woman slit his throat, blood spraying his golden armor.

"I'm fine, Justine," Privia insisted as the rebel leader wiped blood from Privia's bruised Elven features. Together, they joined the battle.

The fighting was fierce but brief. Afterward, the victors penned the last of the High Elves in the town square like hogs on market day.

Privia stood nearby, watching as the beautiful rebel leader delivered their ultimatum. "You can stay, but you'll take your turn in the fields," Justine told the surviving High Elves. "No more hoarding wealth, while others starve."

"Unacceptable!" bellowed the King.

"Then leave. When you inform your kin in other towns that a band of inferior Humans and low caste Elves defeated you, will those High Elves take you in? Share their wealth?"

Discord grew among the captives. "The King no longer speaks for us," shouted an Elven woman in a mud-spattered gown. "We'll work."

Body aching, Privia limped over to stand by Justine, watching the King's world crumble. He glared through the barricade. "Why, Privia? You were my favorite daughter."

Justine took Privia's hand as they turned away. They had food stores to share, wealth to redistribute, two vastly different peoples to unite.

Love has a way, Privia thought, squeezing Justine's hand, *of making us see as others see.*

DOUGH CAT
DEVON WIDMER (299 WORDS)

Honorable Mention

Dough squelched between Marlena's knuckles as she kneaded. *Too sticky,* she thought and sprinkled a few pinches of flour.

Marlena baked more by whim than recipe, and yet, as if by magic, every loaf she crafted came out light, flakey, and absolutely delicious—or at least so she'd been told. Marlena usually baked to share. But today, she needed an entire comfort loaf all to herself.

As she pounded the dough, Marlena couldn't help but imagine she was punching Bob Pemberton (repeatedly) in the nose. "You're starting to become a crazy old cat lady minus the cats." That's what Bob had said to her when she declined to go out for drinks with him after work. Marlena'd been dealing with ignorant comments about being aroace since middle school, but even now that she was pushing forty, they still pissed her off. Ironically, she'd always *adored* cats. The only reason she didn't own one was fear of comments like Bob's.

Fortunately, there was something soothing about shaping a batch of perfectly pillowy dough. Marlena pinched, patted, and molded in a kind of trance. Before long, she realized she'd formed the dough into the shape of a cat. With a shrug, she left the dough cat on the counter to rise.

❧

"Mrow."

Wide-eyed, Marlena gripped the edge of the counter to prevent herself from dropping to the floor. Her dough was—meowing? She reached out a tentative hand. The dough cat stretched up to headbutt her palm.

So. Soft. A dough cat. If she baked it, would it become a bread cat—or a dead cat? Marlena couldn't possibly take the chance. She rubbed the squishy, slightly sticky kitty beneath the chin and got a cheerful "Mrp" in response.

Dough cat it was. Marlena couldn't help but smile. *Her* dough cat.

AND STILL I RISE

O.E. TEARMANN (298 WORDS)

And still I rise
They've got us cornered. Nowhere to go.
And still I rise
Dove glances at me, dark eyes ringed in fear-white. My sweet Dove.
Till death do us part. We both made that promise.
I thought we'd get to keep it longer.
They're saying something about *dykes*, and *freaks*, and worse. I'm not going to listen.
And still I rise
They've got baseball bats. And they've got chains. And they've got those grins. The slap of metal on skin cracks off the alley walls.
They're not starting right away. They're taking their time. Catcalling. Making it last.
Bastards.
And still I rise
Dove's soft hand is cold in mine.
And still I rise
How did it go again?

> *With your bitter, twisted lies*
> *You may trod me in the very dirt*
> *But still, like dust, I'll rise*

Words like wingbeats. Maya Angelou spoke like one of the Igbo. I don't know if she was one of us or not, but she sure could sing our song.
Maybe she *could* rise.

They're getting close. The bricks are rough against my back. Pinpricks burn along my shoulders.

"Hawk?"

I give sweet Dove a squeeze, watching the Hetero Humanity assholes circle. My muscles shake, but my voice is smooth.

"Dove. Let's rise."

"You sure?"

"Yeah baby. I am."

Dove's breath is loud. Even over the sound of men promising they'll 'teach you bitches how to take a dick", I hear it.

Breaths like wingbeats.

And still I rise.

My shoulder blades shift.

"Rise, Dove baby."

Finally, Dove's sweet voice replies. "Rise."

Our wings shine as they unfurl, spread like ink. Wingbeats like words, telling our story. A story that doesn't end here. Shimmer-onyx feathers can write us something better.

Together, Dove and I crouch.

And leap.

And *rise*.

FALLING UPWARD INTO STARLIGHT

JENDIA GAMMON (294 WORDS)

Radiadne tried to let go and allow the warm updraft to carry her upward, but her wings instinctively pulsed in panic. She closed her pewter eyes, feeling the familiar dizziness of anxiety spin through her. She swallowed.

Pelter watched through slitted, teal eyes, their eyelids bronze bespeckled with green, and clucked their tongue. Pelter had coached Radiadne through her tense nerves many times, but today was a crucial test for all fairies of age. The sapphire cliffs of the land of Drillenwe provided the final flight exam to graduate with a master's in updraft gliding. The problem was, Radiadne could not glide; she could only flail, and spring skittishly back to the cliff.

"You'll never get a family this way, Radiadne," her mother had cautioned during her last failed attempt. "Look at your sister: three fine grandchildren she's given me! What you'll be, goodness knows."

Radiadne sighed. She and Pelter enjoyed their quiet relationship. Pelter was a golden fairy with green wings, and she was lavender with fire-hued wings. Neither needed any traditional validation for their future; they simply *were*.

"You're thinking about your mom again." Pelter clucked again. "Just. Breathe. It's fine to feel dizzy; breathe through it, and you won't panic. Breathe through it. I'll join you."

So Radiadne stood at the edge of the sapphire cliffs and stared at Pelter. Pelter breathed in through their nose and out through their mouth slowly and deeply.

"I don't need the destiny anyone else imagines for me," whispered Radiadne. Pelter grinned and nodded, teal eyes shining. Radiadne pumped her wings, then flew backward, as if floating on water. The updraft caught her, and she sailed skyward, smiling. Pelter soon glided alongside her, just as the first stars shone through the violet and indigo twilight.

DANCE OF THE PHOENIX
EVELYN BENVIE (300 WORDS)

"I've grown tired of these matters," the Queen Tyrant says, waving her fawning ministers away. "You, dancing girl. Entertain me."

Mai's breath catches in her throat. *Finally. Finally, the time has come.*

She rises from within the shadow of a column and spins into the center of the room. Her red scarves trail behind her like wings. The delicate scent of peonies lingers in the air around her from the special perfume her clothes are soaked in. Her skin is oiled to silken perfection, for dancing girls should always look soft and smell nice.

She dances. Her body is a thing of beauty to behold, and the Queen Tyrant beholds it ravenously, beckoning her closer. Mai dances to her, bare feet pounding on the red carpet leading to the throne. Up the steps to the dais, body bending and swaying in supplication before her Queen Tyrant.

The Queen Tyrant demands her closer still, dragging Mai in by one of her errant scarves. Dragging Mai, still dancing, back to her royal chambers. Mai doesn't—can't—stop dancing. Her Queen Tyrant has not given her permission.

That's alright. It's part of her plan.

The candlelight makes her red dress glow like flames. Her scarves move like wildfire. She casts them across the room, mesmerizing her Queen Tyrant. It's easy to slip close to her. Wrap a scarf around her shoulder, dip it down to brush against her breasts. Cast another across the room, floating in the air until the very end grazes the nearest candle's flame. And like a fuse being lit, fire tears through it.

Perfume and oil burn so quickly, and so hot. Mai embraces her Queen Tyrant as the flame engulfs them, knowing that in the ashes of her sacrifice, a new day will finally dawn for her people.

DEAD NAME

SORREN BRIARWOOD (300 WORDS)

Winner - Second Place

Ash had never killed anyone—not even consensually.
"Would you get on with it? The water's cold."
"Last chance to back out." Ash tried for a grin.
A pair of steady hands found their shaky ones in the dark.
"I trust you, love."
Ash took a salt-sharp breath.

WHEN THE HARBOURMASTER'S eldest had sought out Ash, they hadn't known what to expect. It hadn't been the words:
"I hear you're a witch. I need you to change me."
Ash regarded the curls tucked underneath the cap, the slouch designed to draw attention from the chest.
"Sorry, handsome," they said, and were rewarded with a startled smile. "I'm a necromancer. Can't change anything unless it's dead."
"Even better."

MONTHS LATER, they stood face-to-face, knee-deep in the ocean. Starlight trembled on the water. Gently, firmly, Ash pushed down. Held on fast through the spasms, the instinctive struggles, until they felt their charge go limp.

Leaving the body floating in the shallows was the difficult part, but it had to look like an accident.

§&

THE FOLLOWING DUSK, Ash watched the funeral from the shoreline, unseen. They winced at the name the mourners wailed, willed the seagulls' cries to drown it.

When the moon crested the horizon, Ash approached the newest grave.

It wasn't difficult for them to reach out with their magic and grasp hold of those bones—they knew them better than their own now. Even easier to reshape the flesh, so eager to be transmogrified: roiling water cresting into a wave.

Ash raised him anew, and the grave dirt crumbled like seafoam.

He stretched, luxuriously, as if waking from a nap, and half-glanced at the headstone.

"Check it out," he grinned, pointing. "My *dead*name."

"You're impossible." Ash took his true face in their hands and kissed him in the pearlescent moonlight.

This one grabs you with its first line and doesn't let go. The judges loved this clever interpretation of the theme, and the fact that it told its story clearly and completely, always a challenge in the flash fiction format. And such a sweet and funny ending.

DEVOTION
ADRIK KEMP (289 WORDS)

Her eyes are heavy with kohl. Hair twisted into configurations others can only imagine, twined around a golden crown. The royal robes of fur are gilt with gemstones in every colour. And her skin drips with gold and diamonds.

I kneel before her immaculate feet, each toenail studded with stones, each curve accentuated by golden threads. As if our Queen is both a doll and sovereign at once. Her voice is fierce however, and the sword that connects us from her right hand to my left shoulder is heavy and powerful.

"Before you now, I, Queen Constantine the Third, ruler of all, do hereby present Henrietta Gorgonheim to my kingdom and all those we lay to waste. Her strength and brutality at war are a lesson and an example to us all."

No hair falls over my lowered face, for it is shorn for war. My body aches from battle and yearns still for more. I am but one of many to be knighted on this day, but in this moment, it is as if we are alone in the atrium.

"Rise, Sir Gorgonheim."

The Queen is revealed before me as I lift my head. Her legs hidden by folds of fur, her waist covered with armour not unlike my own, but brilliant with diamonds. Her chest, full and firm. Her shoulders and arms, strong and muscular. And her fierce, set lips, strong nose and piercing brown eyes that meet with mine for an electrifying moment.

A moment in which I want nothing more than to feel her lips on mine, her hands beneath my armour and her voice at my ear.

"You honour me, my Queen. I am now and always will be, yours."

For this, is devotion.

SURRENDER TO THE SKY
RODELLO SANTOS (296 WORDS)

Honorable Mention

And he was there, rising like the dawn, to hover outside my skyscraper apartment. This high, a sudden gust made his white cape wave. A mockery of surrender, my bitter heart said.

The window was open, but he waited. I nodded him entry, cursing the tremors of hope that wracked me.

"Hello, James," he said, as if years had not passed, as if the cracks of a broken heart had miraculously healed.

I flinched, recalling his cold denial that day, my choked fury. "I know you feel the same," I had pleaded.

"You're wrong," he said then, but eyes that could pierce through walls and unleash the heat of novae could not meet my own. His cape had fluttered while he rose, up, up...away from me. Except for the tv and newspapers, it had been the last I'd seen of him until now.

He looked around, inspecting my apartment, glancing everywhere but at me. He pulled *Ascension* from my bookcase, the biography I'd written on him, a bestseller. From Chapter 20, he read:

"*'If the mind of so godly a being is unknowable, then how can his heart not be likewise impenetrable? Does he grieve, or rejoice, immeasurably? Could one fathom the gulf of his regrets? Can he love—'*"

"—as mortals love?" I asked.

His eyes rose finally from the book to meet mine, and our gazes held each other.

"*All* grief defies measure," he whispered. "*All* regret. And only from mortals can a god truly learn to love. Forgive me, James. You were *never* wrong."

He drew closer, reaching out, and a strength that could shatter mountains, that could nudge moons astray, lifted me dreamlike.

He carried me outside, gently. As the world fell and fell and fell away, we surrendered to the sky.

ACE-TRAL PROJECTION

MINERVA CERRIDWEN (299 WORDS)

The Bewitched Quiltbag Pride Festival was fast approaching. Every year I longed to participate in the Parade of Marvels, but I'd never had an idea good enough to be selected. Until now. Or so I'd thought.

"Come down!" Nousta yelled in my ear, hundreds of miles away.

"I don't know how!"

The dragon was ascending higher and higher above the mountain. At first I had thought the creature was traveling to xyr lair, but as xe advanced to great heights where freezing air was burning my eyes—xyr eyes—that seemed unlikely. I couldn't control xem; I could only undergo the beating of my wings, climbing ever further.

Granted, if one were to project one's spirit into the body of a majestic dragon to make an impression on their fellow asexuals, one should probably research how to retract said spirit to their own body *before* the experiment. One just *might* be an impulsive bundle of hyperfocuses in an overexcited trench coat, and that's how Nousta was left in the Projections lab with a crystal ball depicting this dragon's flight, my empty physical shell, and an abundance of panic. She was muttering incantations to summon me back, but I stopped listening when the dragon looked down at last, offering me a distant yet astonishing view of tree-top patterns and lakes gilded by sunlight.

"Did you really think I wouldn't notice?" xe rumbled.

I was so startled that xe almost lost balance in the sky.

"I'll expel your spirit back to that small human body you're yearning for," the dragon continued.

"A body *I* am yearning for? That's a first."

The dragon huffed disapprovingly. "In the future, please think better about possessing sentient creatures."

I decided against telling xem about the rising trend of people spending their holidays in cat form.

TRUST
ERIN JAMIESON (296 WORDS)

We shiver in lace ball gowns, trains trailing in freshly fallen snow.

"Where are we?" Kendra asks, adjusting her veil over box braids.

I don't answer, struck by the beauty of her hazel eyes, the soft glow that tells me she's ready to cast a spell.

That she understands, like I do, that we're in danger.

I cast a simple illumination spell, casting light on a snow-capped mountain at dawn. Of all the places I teleported, this was not wise. Lace illusion sleeves may look dreamy for exchanging vows, but they do nothing to protect us from vitriolic wind.

Footprints. Boot footprints, all the same size.

They followed us here- even though I thought we left in time, just before we became wife and wife.

I inhale sharp air that burns in my chest and throat. Kendra is still learning to control her magic.

"We have to go," I urge. "Teleport somewhere else."

"Teleport again? But they're already here. They'll follow us."

Before I can answer, Kendra kisses me full on the mouth. "You have to trust me."

Cries in the distance. All men, burly, leather capes. Coming not to kill, but place us under their servitude. Men who believe women should not learn magic.

Kendra casts a fire spell, flames erupting against snow. I dodge a rush of gold, narrowly missing a stunning spell.

Kendra cries out. She fails to cast another spell.

"Try something else!" I scream, tripping over my wedding train.

She grabs my hand.

I close my eyes and grip hard.

A flying spell, one neither of us have ever attempted. At first we dip, and I think we'll fall, but the warmth of her fingers grows, and we rise, up over the mountains, until the men below us are inconsequential specks.

FAIRY DUST
CLAIRE DAVON (283 WORDS)

When I saw the boy, I braced myself for the taunts. They weren't long in coming.

"Fatty, fatty, you're a little batty."

Lionel Hampstead never understood why I wouldn't go out with him. Three years ago, I hadn't had the words to tell him that he wasn't my type—but his sister Regina was.

The time he'd caught me in the marshy area behind our houses still lingered in my mind. The bruises had faded, but not the memories.

"Leave me alone, Lionel."

His face, like his sister's and yet different, twisted.

"Loser. I bet they shipped you off to that camp because you're a freak." He sidled to me, his boldness growing with every step.

I'd matured into my power late. When the time had come, my parents sent me to our relatives to teach me things Lionel would never understand.

That's what happened in faerie.

When he got close enough, I unfurled my wings and grabbed him, shooting into the air.

His confidence shifted to panic at once. "Put me down! Help!"

I hoped Regina would like the change—she always said she preferred interesting people. Wind whipped our hair around as I flew higher. Lionel shrieked, the sound piercing.

"Never torment me again. If you tell a soul about this, I'll drop you off the cliff outside of town."

I fluttered to the ground, and released him. Lionel staggered away from me, his face a mask of fear.

"Freak." Lionel spit the word before he broke and ran.

I returned my wings to their secret place along my back. Time to call a certain someone and see if she wanted to go out tonight.

Even a fairy had to eat.

THE EXPERIMENTAL WITCH
ANUSHA ASIM (300 WORDS)

There were many things that people thought were wrong with Maya. For one, she was an unmarried woman with no desire to change it. She had tried to explain that love and sensuality were things she just didn't have the capacity for but that didn't help. People suggested she was possessed by an evil spirit, cursed by someone she had wronged...the theories were endless. At the age of twenty-five, when the village aunties told her she was nearing her expiration date, Maya made a decision. If people wanted to associate the supernatural with her, she might as well give them what she wanted.

Vampirism was too gory, while diluting her form to a ghost would get monotonous so witchcraft, it was. The art of her female ancestors whose voices had been stifled. The power found in joining nature with the mind.

Maya had just started to share this power. She brewed potions to induce infertility in housewives who were pressured to incubate offspring for their husbands and families. She excelled at this.

Her spells, however, were experimental. Maya had repeated this warning to her last customer but they were desperate. After drinking up, they disintegrated into nothing.

She knew the village elders had deemed her demonic, but this incident had to be the last straw. So that night, when she was being followed by a strange man, Maya knew they wanted her dead. She halted suddenly, clutching the knife she was hiding under her dupatta.

"Maya!" called out the man. At first he was unrecognizable but then the smile that lit up his face made the cogs in her memory spin. His warm hazel eyes only confirmed what she suspected.

He pointed to his flat chest. "I'm in the right body now,"

Maya grinned. Her spells could work after all.

SCIENCE FICTION PART TWO

Maybe it wasn't a good idea to build a drive-in on the old A-bomb test site, but the land was dirt cheap and glowed in the dark, which saved immeasurably in lightning expense.

— DEAN WELLS, *IT CAME FROM ATOM CITY*

IT CAME FROM ATOM CITY
DEAN WELLS (300 WORDS)

Judge's Choice - Ben Lilley

Maybe it wasn't a good idea to build a drive-in on the old A-bomb test site, but the land was dirt cheap and glowed in the dark, which saved immeasurably in lightning expense.

But in the days that followed the opening gala, one and all in the sleepy desert town started to lose molecular cohesion and melt, and folks concluded that, no, the idea was probably not a good one after all.

Mrs. Nussbaum decohesed over her brisket at Fat Man and Little Boy's. Cecil Wade decohesed in the clinic as he turned his head and coughed. Leo DeLucca decohesed while fishing and was eaten by black crappies. And poor Miss Eula Bliss flushed herself as she decohesed in the teacher's loo at Enola Gay High.

So, when delivery boy lanky Chip Stankey began to feel moist, and much more so than was usual, he knew the sorry end was near.

Now Chip was smitten with Endless Ted Cavalina, a soda jerk from the wrong side of the tracks. No one knew, least of all Ted. The boy filled a need that Chip had never shared with anyone. But awkward glances were all that transpired between them, and his smittenness remained unfulfilled.

Chip woke in the early hours of the morning to find Endless Ted on his stoop; hands in threadbare pockets, kicking a stone.

Something was different. Ted was different. A choice had been made; Chip felt it, that and the excessively damp bedsheet wrapped around his waist.

Endless Ted was saying goodbye, and Chip knew the day would be their first as well as their last.

No words were spoken, no confessions of longing or love. They simply kissed and held one another close when decohesion finally came, and ascended together as mist in the rising desert sun.

It has been my extreme pleasure to judge Queer Sci Fi's Annual Flash Fiction Anthology Contest year after year. This year, I have claimed It Came From Atom City as my judge's pick. A classic tale of unrequited love with a moving–and surprisingly humorous at times–sci-fi spin, It Came From Atom City combined environmentalism and the awkwardness of queer love into a humorous and compelling story with a happy-enough ending. This delightful piece of flash fiction was ranked highly by our judges; I simply happened to be the one to snap it up first as my judge's pick.

—Ben Lilley

LIFTOFF
EF DEAL (289 WORDS)

Three of Delia's arms wrangled the controls between explosive sparks in the circuitry. Her fourth arm held the door loosely against tinks against the hull from the indigenous tribe's primitive weaponry, awaiting Captain Nix's return, holding out hope Nix survived the barrage and managed to get safely back to the module.

Nix's scent wafted in, along with her child's. A sudden drumming on the door indicated an uptick in the attack. The door was yanked from Delia's grasp and Nix dove into the module, huddled around an unwieldy bundle. Delia slammed the door, then gently unrolled the pack.

Nix caught her appendage in a desperate grip. "They thought he was food."

Delia caressed her brow reassuringly as she peeled back the blanket and kissed the infant boy's tiny face scrunched with displeasure.

Nix pulled herself up to sit, gripping her left leg above a blackened patch on her pants. "I think it might be poison." She wagged her head dizzily. "Can't feel my foot. Amputate before it spreads."

Delia set the baby in Nix's lap and glided to the door, one arm taking on the silver cast of the module's hull. She cautiously cracked the door to slide a hand-like appendage along the hull to the ground and plucked up one of the missiles to examine. Nix opened her shirt to nurse her son while Delia ran the weapon through a spectrometer.

"Bacteria," she pronounced. "You won't lose your leg. Ysir won't lose his mothers."

Delia prepared a hypo and applied it. She remolded her amorphous form to enfold Nix who snuggled into her embrace, still cradling Ysir.

Nix gazed gratefully up into Delia's eyestalks. "Do we have liftoff?"
Delia formed human lips to kiss her. "We do now."

OUR TRUE SELVES INCARNATE

ELLERY ARDEN (300 WORDS)

"You won't feel a thing," the technician reassures us. She scans my Mirror Chip, then Alex's. "Test the connection."

I touch Alex's hand. We gasp, looking at our hands in confusion, a bubble of excitement stirring free from its place deep within us.

❧

ALONE IN THE ADJACENT ROOM, Alex and I reach for each other. An arm encircles a waist; a fingertip explores a wrist. With each touch, we experience both perspectives—the touching and the touched. I kiss down Alex's neck, from their ear to their shoulder. I shiver, smiling at the paradox of feeling my lips on my own neck.

When it's perfected, I'm sure this technology will find its niche with people like us. People who transcend the binary.

Alex traces their fingertips along my collarbone. We sigh in unison. But it's not fingers, not collarbones, that we are here to touch.

Two hours of connection. Two hours to explore that which the other possesses.

We fall onto the bed, my hand between their legs, their hand between mine. A hand on a cock, a finger in a cunt. Stroking, probing.

We feel each other's parts as extensions of our bodies, the Mirror Chip technology connecting our nervous systems so that we may truly live within each other's skin for this brief time.

I can feel our finger in our cunt, and our hand on our cock. When I close my eyes, I no longer remember which parts I was born with and which are mine for just two hours.

Bubbles of euphoria pop between us as we writhe. As the intensity rises, a tear falls from Alex's eye. I understand its meaning because I feel it too. This experience is more than connected neurons and a flood of endorphins. We are now our true selves incarnate.

IT STARTED WITH A BRICK

ROXANNE SKELLY (289 WORDS)

Honorable Mention

Some say it was Marsha "Pay it no mind." To others, it was Miss Silvia. But a hundred years have passed since someone let it fly. Maybe there wasn't no brick, just a shot glass, or quarters and pennies, tossed as they dragged Stormé away. But that was a different time, when the cops fell, and the Wall stood strong. When the ground moved with the stomping of a hundred, or two hundred, a thousand angry feet.

And that time is now. This very night. And I'm here, me, just another queen, a nameless trans woman, still smelling of ozone and anxiety from the temporal shift. Here to record a history that they'd tried so hard to erase. Recovering yet another piece of a lost past, to rebuild who we are, who we will be.

Stormé yells as them uniformed thugs drag her away. "Loosen these cuffs, pig!" Her voice shatters the night as pain twists her stone-butch face.

Then the baton does what batons do when held by power, and down she falls to her knees. I feel it too. The pain. Just watching it is enough.

Marsha P., fist raised beside me, pays it mind. So do the other queens and barflies. Ain't nobody messes with Stormé. Quarters fly. Nickels and dimes too. Shouts of "let her go."

My blood catches fire, the same spark of rage that'd kindled in me when I volunteered to enter the Well. These are my people. This is my history. I own this, as does every fucking queer across the centuries.

The shouts of my siblings fill me. They drive me.

I kneel.

I wrap my palm around it.
I stand.
The brick leaves my fingers.
And time calls me home.

UPLOADED
STACEY MAHUNA (299 WORDS)

Honorable Mention

It used to be that the dying hoped for heaven. Now, they choose their own. Most of the time.

"Cam," my brother whispers from his hospital bed. His congregation, his wife and his kids have spent the last hour assuring him they'll see him in paradise, the *real* paradise. The one I Upload people into, the one with endless lines of code and pre-configured bliss, is an abomination.

As a company liaison, it's my job to sift through the minds of the dying, annotate their heavenly requirements, prepare their Requested Immortality Server Entry, and gather the data. Then I upload their RISE forms to Cloud Nine. Most people choose it over oblivion. My brother is old school. Never could spare a minute for his gay, atheist, techie sister.

"Rob," I mutter. "Why am I here?"

"I need to..." he coughs. He's more sarcoma than human now, and as he flutters like a broken bird, I swallow back the tears. "...tell you something. Please." He motions me down, putting paper thin gray lips to my reluctant ear.

When he's finished, the breath leaves him like a long sigh and I am left reeling.

The RISE form is under his pillow. On it is scribbled an unfamiliar name. *Robyn*. It's the name he's—she's? —buried from the world this entire time. The one unable to be spoken aloud, even at the end. I stuff it under my shirt.

When the AI can't match your RISE form with a birth record, you still get Uploaded, just randomized. You might wake up in a new body, alone, in an unfamiliar place. Some might find it terrifying.

Some might ask for it as their dying wish.

I already know what I'll do. After all, it's paradise. You can be anyone you want.

COMMIT

SONJA SEREN CALHOUN (298 WORDS)

Honorable Mention

A soft chime pierces through the viscous fluid. My body flinches out of surprise. After what feels like weeks without any sense of gravity, or physicality, it's reassuring. The chime reminds me that I am more than a mind in an egg of my own making.

My eyes are closed. It's the only way to ignore media feeds, and biometrics. A bright light prompts me to open them.

I see a white screen with black text.

Final Session

Do you consent?: Y/N

I've had months to think. Soaking in this bath of hormones, nanites and amniotic fluid. Being slowly softened like clay. Months of living through a media visor. Presenting "my best self" online. Whatever or whoever that is.

The pressure is immense. Do I keep my genitals? Breasts? Hair? What gender am I?

I want to ignore the prompt forever.

My grandmother's stories come back to me. The years of therapy. Irreversible surgeries. Hiding the things medicine and scalpels couldn't erase. Back then they made you commit and make do.

Now? I could do this again. Another three months. But does that make all of this less valid?

"When I woke up and saw nothing between my legs? Never cried so hard in my life. I had no regrets. I felt whole."

Grandma's words wrap around me. I don't have to be the best gender. I just have to be the best me.

Do you consent?: Y

The distant pinch of needles is followed by the display shifting to a cascading fractal. Within it I can see a human form. The form I am telling the medicine and machines to shape.

In a day's time I will emerge from the tank. I will know exactly who I am. I will cry with joy like my grandmother did.

UNDERGROUND TO THE STARS
T. D. CARLSON (298 WORDS)

It hurt keeping his eyes cast down and away from the stars. No one's eyes in New Richwood reflected the lights from so far above, and as the firstborn son of Pastor Briscett, Zachariah was expected to keep it that way. He was slated to take up the mantle of priesthood when he came of age. He'd been raised to rule the hearts of his people, keep them faithful and close to home, never leaving Earth.

On a mission to save souls, Zach bumped shoulders with a man on a crowded sidewalk and turned to apologize. The man smiled at him and tilted his head just so when their eyes met. There were universes glittering in the other man's eyes. Week after week, conversation after conversation, then touch after touch, Liam became his world.

Until his father found out. The cleansing by flail began. So many lashes.

Here he was, finally, too far for his father to reach. Beyond home, beyond family, beyond everything. He couldn't stop the anxious shivers running through him as the lift took him higher. It'd taken an old concept called an 'underground railroad' to get him here. He'd escaped Earth, bounced from a waystation above Mars, and onto a freight liner that dropped him off at his new home. A beautiful, hope-filled station far from Earth with connective rings and spokes and all ranges of fantastic life existing within it. One of those lives would be his starry-eyed Liam waiting for him when the nearly silent lift finished its ascent.

Zach tapped impatient hands on his thighs as the lift slowed to a stop and the doors slid to either side. Liam, with an ear-splitting grin and sparkling brown eyes, waited with open arms. Zach knew those arms would never let him go.

THE SEVEN MILLION

PATRICIA LOOFBOURROW (300 WORDS)

Honorable Mention

I was born on the way to Mt. Everest. After my mother died, Mama took me with her.

But I should start at the beginning.

We'd poisoned ourselves down to seven billion before the Yoronoti came.

They offered a new home. The first seven million to arrive at their ship, parked on our tallest mountain, would be taken there.

But there were conditions.

We must take the trip by foot, carrying any provisions with our own hands. We must use no violence along the way. And we must step into the ship on our own volition.

The rich men, of course, flew up, and were shot down. Others hired men to carry their belongings. These were returned to their homes (teleporting, they called it), while those carrying the packs were offered the choice to enter.

Most of the others fought and clawed, raped and murdered their way to the gates, only to be cast over the side of the mountain.

By then many stopped trying, believing the journey too dangerous, unwilling to leave their homes and babies behind.

Some gave up midway, penniless, exhausted. Still more camped along the route to prey on the travelers, or to supply those passing.

That last is how we survived.

My mother was a climber of mountains. She and Mama met along a dirt road near Kathmandu. My mother helped Mama survive.

I have no recollection of her. But Mama's voice told me of the love they'd had together.

I remember that last rise, the ship's wide entryway. The six and all those nines.

Mama gasped, shuddered. Then she said, "I'll race you! Let's run in together."

I ran inside to cheers!

A door slammed shut behind. Terrified, I ran to the clear plass.

Mama stood below, smiling through tears, watching my ship rise.

EITHER-OR ANSWERS AFTER SALLY RIDE

X. HO YEN (298 WORDS)

"Does your species still reproduce by uncontrolled genetic exchange?"

Until now the Encyclopedia Galactica access questions were uncontroversial.

"Ohh, ho ho," Sydney laughed, momentarily fogging their spacesuit helmet.

"No problem," said Sam, poking gloved fingers through the virtual 'yes' button on the kiosk's display.

"Does your species still have preferential social constructs associated with sexual reproduction? (genetic mating type role mystiques, parent role mystiques, devaluing of gender and sex variations from the reproductive mating types, etc.)"

"Ho ho heh heh hoooooo," Sydney laughed. "Come on, cis/hetero, spin that for the big teddy bear."

"This is crazy. What do our social constructs have to do with..." Sam started to say.

Sydney's nose aimed down and a bit to the side. Their eyebrows went up.

"Gaining access to the most powerful knowledge base imaginable?" they said. "Gathered by uncounted advanced species over millions, possibly billions of years?"

"Okay," said Mission Control, watching through cameras and listening. "Cut the sarcasm, please."

The E.G. access portal kiosk had been uncovered by lunar digger robots. When Sam and Sydney were sent to check it out, it scanned them at least well enough to detect deception. Then it started a timer and insisted that only they could answer the qualification questionnaire, with no remote cuing.

The galactic-scale uplift of humanity was on them alone.

Sam blinked and sweated.

"You can't lie to it, Sam," said Sydney. "You know the answer."

Sam pressed the virtual 'yes' button.

"Final question," responded the portal kiosk. "Which mating type, if any, contributes counterbalancing Ubuntu?"

Sam's eyes widened. Sydney looked away, frowning.

"What do we say?" said Sam. "What do we say?"

Sydney sighed. "My people get this shit on forms all the time."

They typed in "Either, both, or neither." Truth.

The kiosk displayed a spinning galaxy icon.

DISCOVERED
CHRIS PANATIER (296 WORDS)

Haoyu gazed up at David. "Tell me a story."

"What kind of story?"

"A love story."

"A love story. Okay," said David.

"Once upon a time, two men from different planets joined the solar services as twenty-somethings. There were thousands of other people just like them, hired on to undertake risky missions to faraway places in search of new planets." David coughed, inhaled deeply, and continued. "They trained for years, separated by millions of miles, never knowing the other existed. At the conclusion of their training, some faceless administrator selected them to crew a mission to an unexplored star.

"The two men couldn't have been more different. One was quiet. The other never shut up."

Haoyu made a rasping laugh.

"One played chess. The other preferred movies. One was sentimental, the other rather stoic.

"After several years, the men found they were often quiet together, then talking nonstop. They played chess over coffee, watched shows before bed. The stoic astronaut observed that he'd never felt happier—that this must mean he was in love. The sentimental astronaut already knew this.

"Years later, they arrived at a virgin star and with it, the perfect planet. They sent word and prepared to deorbit and land. It would be theirs alone for six years.

"But there was a problem with the life support. It was failing, and shockingly fast.

"Carbon dioxide saturated the air. The stoic astronaut asked the sentimental astronaut if it was a romantic notion or a horrific one that just by breathing they were killing each other. The sentimental astronaut said it would be romantic if they lived to see their first sunrise together, horrific otherwise."

The limb of the planet began to glow. Haoyu wheezed. David kissed him on the cheek and held his breath.

FROM STASIS
GRACE HUDSON (295 WORDS)

Honorable Mention

"She's awake."

Bright colors flash at the corners of my eyes. Needles of light stab at my cones and rods. I can't feel my legs. In fact, I can't feel anything. Maybe I died. I can't remember anything about before. There's only my mind, and colors.

The beep comes from somewhere near my right ear, followed by a hissing sound.

"Riga of Barelon, arise." His voice is deep, and somehow familiar. My palms hit a solid wall, some kind of hybrid plastic. I'm sure I know what this is. Maybe I designed it. The colors won't go away, no matter how much I blink.

"Where am I?"

"It's the stasis gas. It will wear off soon enough." My vision swims, blurring his features. I can only make out his beard. Another face flashes behind my eyes, dark blue eyes, spiky blonde hair. My world.

"Gita? Where is she?"

"Your girlfriend is in pod seven-two-one. Thankfully safe and sound." Another hissing sound, but it's just my breath escaping. The air tastes sweeter now.

There's something he's not saying. His face scrunches into a grimace.

"It's Neils, isn't it?" He nods as I mutter my apologies for forgetting his name. "What about the pods in section nine and ten?"

He glances past me, his eyes ringed with red and I know. I already know.

"They're dead, aren't they?"

Nobody speaks. I want to see Gita. Why won't they let me see her? I hear her voice crying out. Now she knows too.

I suck in air and focus. "The captain?" Neils nods. "The tech crew? Everyone?"

Then it hits me.

"What did you call me before? When I woke up?"

"Riga of Barelon." He salutes, expectant eyes meeting mine, and now I understand.

He's awaiting captain's orders.

SPEAKING UP
BEÁTA FÜLÖP (189 WORDS)

Honorable Mention

I always loved raising my hand in school. Having the answer. Asking to be heard, begging for approval. The teacher only called on me as a last resort, and even then, what I had to say was wrong, my stories too wild, my poems too colorful.

I never left school, not really. I'm still there in my dreams, raising my hand, hoping to answer a question, to prove myself. Always the teacher asks for somebody else.

It's different out here, among the stars. We don't talk about literature much. But now we do. Now, it is the whole crew assembled, asked who could recite a poem for the alien ambassadors. It is important. They asked for it, their requirements specific, and it took as all by surprise.

The mass hall is silent, just as it was in the classroom.

The ambassadors want something good, but also something fun. Something gay, in both senses of the word.

Too wild, the teacher inside of me whispers. *Too wild, too colorful.*

The crew avoids looking at the Captain, stares at their feet.

And I raise my hand.

HORROR

Sonny tiptoed through the kitchen at 3 am. Their tummy grumbled when they saw the chocolate bunny on the counter awaiting slaughter. Alas, they couldn't be the one to eat it. Caffeine and sugar were big NOs for Sonny. Sensitive stomach.

Eating that bunny would be a terrible idea.

— ANDREA STANET, *LATE NIGHT RISER*

DARKRISE

RHIAN WALLER (299 WORDS)

Honorable Mention

The shadows first come the day they nervously, deliciously, kiss behind the gymnasium.

Myra worries this is the darkness of sin gathering in folds at the limits of her vision. They talk a lot about sin at school. She always imagines it as something that follows you, like a stench.

"We can stop," said Beryl, when she felt her friend tremble, but Myra doesn't want that. Beryl, always slightly dishevelled, with one sock ruckled lower than the other, her hair frizzing free from the ribbon, is the sunrise of her heart.

They sit together at Assembly, and Myra tries not to shine so bright the whole school sees it. They touch, ankle to ankle in Latin, braiding each other's hair at break, in ways that should go unnoticed as girlishness.

During Needlework, Myra rubs her eyes, but she cannot banish the coalescing dark.

After they suffer through hockey, Mr. Scott enters the changing room and says, "Beryl, Myra, stay behind."

Myra's stomach plunges.

"I saw you," says Mr. Scott, when the last girl leaves.

"Saw us what?" says bold Beryl.

"Your parents and teachers would be so ashamed. God in Heaven, you're fourteen, and already lost."

"Please," says Myra, horrified.

"It could be our secret." He licks his lips. "Kiss," he says, his fingers wandering up his thighs. "Here. Now."

Beryl reaches and Myra takes her hand. The darkness hardens and she recognises it not as sin, but as the other side of their light.

She calls it up. She feels it rise, sees its spreading wings mantle the teacher. Its roar is a kindness covering the sound of snapping sinew and wetly parting muscle. When it departs, the roof rains down.

The gym is closed for six months to repair the ceiling and the accident is never explained.

DAISY COURAGE
PAUL WILSON (300 WORDS)

Honorable Mention

Peeking through the blinds, Daisy watched the zombies. Across the dirt road Sean's trailer remained dark but be damned if she would let the dead stop her. It had taken courage to admit who she was, it had taken courage to go out in public in make-up, and it had damn sure taken courage to tell Sean she loved him—just not as much courage because she knew he loved her too.

'Me' became 'we'...

But now she needed new courage. She needed the grit that let David become Daisy.

She had to get to Sean, but the zombies were thick. She would have to run between them and get inside his door before she got grabbed. It was the end of the world and she wanted to be with her man.

From the television: "The dead continue to rise..."

She would need to rise, too. She was terrified, but she remembered how Sean had stood up to the bullies during their first date. He rose out of his chair and asked them what was so damn funny.

Sean had risen. She could do no less for him.

Daisy gripped the knob and prepared to open her door.

I'll have to run. If his door is locked, I'll have to correct quickly. Maybe try the back door. Oh Sean, I hope you're ready for me, baby.

Daisy yanked open the portal—and gasped because Sean was on her top step. Then she saw the bite on his arm, the grey of his skin.

"NO!"

Sean lunged and grabbed her. He pulled her towards his yawning mouth.

Rise! Use that Daisy courage!

Daisy pushed him away and slammed the door.

Not 'we' now but 'me'...

Daisy cried, but she did so standing up.

LATE NIGHT RISER
ANDREA STANET (299 WORDS)

Sonny tiptoed through the kitchen at 3 am. Their tummy grumbled when they saw the chocolate bunny on the counter awaiting slaughter. Alas, they couldn't be the one to eat it. Caffeine and sugar were big NOs for Sonny. Sensitive stomach.

Eating that bunny would be a terrible idea.

And what would Yasmina say when she found out her Easter basket had been devoured by some wandering beast in the night? Although wandering beast wouldn't be *entirely* inaccurate, Sonny obviously couldn't devour a gift and then admit to it.

They breathed in the bitterness of the cacao tempered by the light hint of milk fat and cane. They ran a finger down the seam at the back of the bunny and leaned down for a deep whiff. Mouth watering, their stomach clenched, warning against a bad decision.

"Sonny? What are you doing up?" Myra dragged her feet until she was in the kitchen doorway, rubbing her eyes much like Yasmina tended to do.

"Nothing!" Sonny's words were muffled. One hand attempted to hold in the brown head, its ear protruding from their mouth.

Myra woke up fully. "No, babe! You didn't!" She huffed, then scowled. "Into the basement. You know you can't eat that stuff after dark!" Of course, Sonny's wife was pissed.

Sonny's head drooped in remorse. They gulped as the first tufts of fur sprouted from their arms. Round ears protruded from the top of their head, and their front teeth protruded from beneath twitching whiskers.

How would Myra explain the situation to Yasmina—that nommy's allergy turned them into a Gremoloshe, a giant rodent with a penchant for mischief. And sweets. "Come on, before you tear up the carpeting again. You'd think you'd have learned some self control by now. Every year, Sonny. Every. Damn. Year."

3X

EMERIAN RICH (300 WORDS)

Sam stumbled over gravestones, pointing her flashlight this way and that.

"Why are we here again?" Kitty asked.

"Because Charm said so."

They'd been in love with Charm. Sam had loved her longer—since she was Charles—but she didn't discount Kitty's connection. Their polyamorous life had seemed like heaven.

"I miss her," Kitty said.

"Me, too." Sam closed her eyes, fighting back tears.

"There it is!" Kitty pointed across the moonlit cemetery to the mausoleum, dwarfing the monuments around it.

Sam rushed ahead and unlocked the decorative gates of the mausoleum. They entered, eyeing the sarcophagus in the center of the space.

"What does it say now?" Kitty asked.

Sam pulled out the note. "Darkness breeds what light forgot. Rise, break forth with what love sought."

"And?"

"That's it."

"Let me see." Kitty grabbed the note. "There's a three X here. Maybe we have to say it three times."

They repeated the rhyme. As the third utterance commenced, a strong wind picked up. They clutched each other under the gale.

The lid of the sarcophagus inched and then blasted aside. Charm rose up, her arms crossed.

Charm was more beautiful than ever, bathed in moonlight, her pale pink robes dappled with colored moonlight streaming through stained glass.

"Help," her voice rasped out.

Kitty shoved Sam out of the way, kissing Charm's ring. Kitty smiled wide, tears streaming. Charm pulled Kitty up into the open sarcophagus.

Sam watched the interaction with fascination. Was it wrong for her to be wary–almost frightened–by the one she'd once shared a bed with?

Charm's gaze was not one of lost love and longing as she pulled young, enthusiastic Kitty in a higher embrace. Her mouth opened wide, exposing a pair of wicked-long canines.

Hunger. Sam thought, and then a second word. *Run!*

IVY, EVERGREEN
MERE RAIN (229 WORDS)

I sit facing the headstone that doesn't bear your name.

You're not dead. James Islington wasn't you. Isn't you.

The parents who chose this stone with its cross and its dead name never knew you. None of them knew you. None of them love you, the real you, the way I do.

That's why I'm the one waiting by your grave at midnight, my heart, my Ivy. Vines tattooed round my arm for your name, ring on my finger for our love.

Bloody corpses circling your grave, lives for your life.

There's nothing I wouldn't do for you, Ivy. No sacrifice too precious, no sin too forbidden. Nothing I won't do to bring you back. I vowed *for better or worse* and for you I would do so much worse than this stolen grimoire, this darkest magic, these bloodstained hands.

A dead name cannot bind you to the land of the dead. I believe this as I call you: *Ivy, rise.*

Around me a thousand gravestones are tumbling as the earth gives up its rotting fruit, but I have eyes only for the movement of the new-turned soil beneath my knees and your bruised fingertips emerging like spring buds.

Let everything go down into the dark, my love. Everything except you. Rise like Persephone conquering winter, like Christ harrowing Hell, like Ragnarok.

I take your cold hand in mine.

THE AWAKENER

TOM FOLSKE (300 WORDS)

Honorable Mention

It's like no one has ever watched a movie before. When a mysterious stranger rolls into town, you wish them well and let them pass. If they find love and decide to stay, you embrace them and they will help the community in its hour of need.

The town of Wind Lake, in northern Minnesota, almost to Canada, was about to experience its hour of need, and instead of helping them, I was to be the cause of their suffering. My name is Denzel Walker, and I come from a long line of necromancers. I am an awakener.

I was planning on passing right through Wind Lake, and maybe everything would have been fine. Then I met Tyler.

Tyler was beautiful in a way reminiscent of Dorian Gray, with a carefree attitude I couldn't help but fall in love with. It was love at first sight for both of us, the mysterious stranger and the free-spirit, and we weren't afraid to show it. According to the internet, this should have been fine. Wind Lake however, was a little behind the times, and some twenty-one-year-old "kids" decided to play a little prank, which led to Tyler, my beloved, being drowned in Wind Lake. They tied him up, brought him out on their boat, and said they only meant to "scare" him, when he "accidentally" slipped and fell in. He was still tied up. He never had a chance. One of the "kids" was the sheriff's son. No charges were ever filed.

Wanna know a fun fact about Wind Lake? It has a big cemetery. I have already helped a couple dozen to rise, and there are plenty more I could awaken. I think what I have will suffice. I just need one more. It will be nice to see Tyler again.

UNDER THE CICADA MOON
TORI THOMPSON (300 WORDS)

Honorable Mention

"I'll make you forget her," the redhead whispered. She dragged Destiny from her barstool and the line of empty shot glasses. The woman led her outside to the parking lot by the hand. "I'll drive. You can barely walk."

Destiny's keys tumbled from her pocket, clanking against the asphalt. Bending over, the redhead retrieved them as Destiny's thirsty eyes drank in her form.

"Like my assets?" Red's smokey voice melted Destiny's insides like lava.

Destiny leaned in for a kiss. Red sidestepped and opened the passenger door, shoving her inside and buckling her in like a child. Glenlivet and sex were perfect panaceas for her heartbreak, she thought as her vision blurred.

৯৯

WHISKY-LADEN SWEAT LACED the glade's aroma as their moonlit bodies grappled on the ground. Arching in pleasure, Destiny screamed. Red silenced her with a crushing kiss. She tasted herself on Red's tongue as she slipped her fingers between her lover's legs.

Red snatched Destiny's hand away. "Let me hold you for a while first."

They gazed upward in each other's arms, watching the waxing gibbous moon's journey.

৯৯

DESTINY AWOKE to one last thrust, wetness dripping between her thighs and Red's body blanketing her. Red met Destiny's befuddled face with large bulging reddish-orange eyes and a smile. Jerking her head away, Destiny flailed against the weight pinning her to the ground as she began to convulse.

"Sh, it'll be over soon. Our eggs are fusing, my darling imago." Red murmured as she caressed Destiny's cheek. "You'll feed our brood, and then they will burrow. In thirty years, our children will re-emerge."

Translucent orange wings unfurled through a rent in Red's back as she sloughed her human shell. The creature launched skyward, fading against the stars as the light disappeared from Destiny's eyes.

Red told her she'd forget.

LILY
KELLY HAWORTH (296 WORDS)

A tombstone stands surrounded by new sod and wilting flowers.

A woman stands beside it, her face buried in her phone.

You try again to get her to leave, to move, to eat. To come home.

"Lily's gone," you say, the words tasting stale.

"Part of her," she corrects, her thumbs tapping, flicking, pausing poised.

Her eyes dart up to meet yours, and you recognize the pursing of her lips.

"I need candles," she says, "and a small knife."

You don't know why you get these things for her. Maybe they'll help her move on.

It's always been easier to let her get what she wants.

"This won't do anything," you say, handing her a bag.

She sets up a circle of candles in front of the tombstone. Their tiny flames dance like stars never could.

"Please, let's go home."

She pricks her finger and lets a few scarlet drops fall into the dirt.

"There is no home without Lily in it," she says. She holds up her phone, and recites.

Her words slip by you as your arguing renews, as you tug at her arm.

Words pull at your ears, but you brush them away, willing the stubborn woman in front of you to return to reality.

"What if it works but it's not really her?"

You feel clever. You're sure she'll stop.

She stares at you. Then through you. To the tombstone.

"Have you loved someone so much you'll die for them? She loved me so much she'll live for me."

You open your mouth to argue, but any defense you conjure falls flat on your tongue.

After all, she's going to get what she wants.

With dawning realization, you turn and run.

"Now rise," she says, holding out her hands.

And Lily does.

FANTASY PART THREE

Nala awoke coughing blood. Her lungs rattled like a serpent's tail, and her heart thudded much too loud. The acrid scent of burnt wood and smoke hit her, mingled with a pleasant undertone of tulips. She breathed slow and deep. Her skin prickled like thorns pressed into her flesh. She was so, so tired. It would be easy to drift back into the darkness.

— KELLIE DOHERTY, *ASHES & TULIPS*

ARTEMIS, FRACTURED
GEORGE UNDERWOOD (297 WORDS)

Honorable Mention
Judge's Choice - Sacchi Green

Artemis approaches the pyre, touches Orion's cold corpse. The earth beneath her feet is soaked with the blood of sacrificed mortals; spiralling patterns etched into the wet ground glow with reflected moonlight. Her spell is almost complete.

'We could have hunted forever,' she says, laying Orion's bow gently on his chest.

The wound that killed him burns raw red upon his neck. Though really, she thinks bitterly, it was jealousy that killed him, that set her brother plotting against them.

She looks to the night sky, where stars burn in the shapes of those the gods have loved and lost. Aquarius, Zeus' waterbearer. Coronis, Apollo's lost love. Memorials they, and the mortals, see every day.

'How could he not have been jealous of what we had?' she whispers. She and Orion had spent millennia as friends, hunting together, laughing together, exploring the world…

God of Virginity, they call her, as if she has put some Herculean effort into it, and it is therefore sacred. As if it were not an innate part of her, unchangeable as the moon. As if she loves to be lonely, and would scorn any kind of companionship just because romance is out of reach.

'You taught me that I could rise above what I was not.'

She steps back.

'Let me return the gift in kind.'

She holds her hands out. The sacrificed corpses spasm; the spiral patterns erupt with light. Flames swallow Orion's body.

'Rise!'

A cloud of glowing sparks drifts from the roaring fire to the black sky above – up, up, up, till they are as distant and bright as the other stars. They settle there in a shining shape, a body achingly familiar to her.

Let the others see that she can love and hurt as hard as them.

Of all the gods of the Greeks, Artemis appeals to me most. A hunter, female but not effeminate. In "Artemis: Fractured", her asexual friendship is deep as any love, and the visual effect of sparks rising in the night sky to become the stars making up the constellation of Orion strikes me as a perfect use of our theme.

—Sacchi Green

ASHES & TULIPS
KELLIE DOHERTY (299 WORDS)

Nala awoke coughing blood. Her lungs rattled like a serpent's tail, and her heart thudded much too loud. The acrid scent of burnt wood and smoke hit her, mingled with a pleasant undertone of tulips. She breathed slow and deep. Her skin prickled like thorns pressed into her flesh. She was so, so tired. It would be easy to drift back into the darkness.

"Open your eyes, Nala," a gentle feminine voice urged. Isla.

Nala's love for Isla burned within her, nudging her awake again. She opened her eyes, wincing at the bright flames beside her. A campfire. Beyond that, night had long since pulled overhead. What happened? Her memory came up blank, and a cold panic shuddered through her.

Then a soft, warm hand pressed onto her cheek, drawing her gaze, and Isla's bright green eyes and gentle smile quelled the rising panic. "I'm glad to see the ritual worked."

"Ritual?" Nala's parched throat burned.

"You died, love. During the battle."

Memories swarmed back like angry bees—Isla pressing a frantic kiss to her lips, battling the bright ones in defense of their simple cottage, her scimitar flashing as she killed one, two, ten…a bright pulse of pain in her chest. The nothing.

Nala blinked. "You drove them away?"

"For now."

Pride washed through Nala at Isla's bravery.

But Isla frowned. "They'll be back. We have what they want."

The egg. The last starlight fox, the bright ones' only true predator and her and Isla's last hope.

Nala sighed. She gripped Isla's hand, pulled herself upright. As she rose, ashes fell around her from the necromantic magic, scattering into the field of pink tulips they kept by their home. She pulled Isla in for a kiss, then grinned. "Then let me show them what death really looks like."

IN THE SHADOW OF YOUR HEART

CHAD GRAYSON (299 WORDS)

For three days, we walked the sundered path, until we came to the precipice, the place where the world wears thin. For half a day, we prepared the singing stones, and, with the crimson blade, you sliced a gash in the wall of the world.

When we first learned of the other worlds, we were boys studying under Sister Celeste. Thrilled by this knowledge, we knew there must be a better world than this. A world where your sister had never been taken by the Sleepers. A world unravaged by the phages. A world where our love did not have to cling to the shadows, but could walk in the light.

The door opened, a seam in the world, haloed in violet flames. With a look back at me you stepped over the edge and passed through.

But then, the baying of the hounds. Nero's hunters had found us. It didn't matter how. I could follow you, but could we seal the rift on the other side?

I scattered the stones and tossed the blade over the edge, sealing the door. The shattered voice that called out "Leander!" still haunts me. You did not understand.

The hounds were upon me, fangs piercing my calf, my shoulder. Nero bound me in barbed wire, shouted questions I wouldn't answer.

And now, Marco, as I wait in chains, my days subject to agony, I regret nothing. More than anything, I needed to keep you safe, no matter what it meant for us. I can still feel you standing between me and the light of creation. You have not left me. I am sheltered in the shadow of your Heart.

And that's how I will find you. When I do, we will rise through the layers of eternity and reach that better world.

URSULA
DAWN SPINA COUPER (299 WORDS)

Honorable Mention

I can't hear the mob over the crash of the waves or the crackling flames. I can't see through the memory of the look on her face, just before they lit the wood beneath her.

§.

I KNEW it was over last night when I saw torch lights in the distance. Just once, I had ignored their calls and knocks and ceaseless pleas for remedies. There was a flash of a face at the window. Someone had seen. Me, breasts bare and wearing men's pants. A councilman's usually unhappy wife, naked in my bed, elated and loved.

They made me watch her burn; They were certain that lighting my fire on the docks and leaving my body for the sea would save them. They didn't know the significance of my home on the beach. They never understood why I allowed the tide to reach my front door. The peculiarities of a witch, they assumed. They did not know that my power came from my mother. But they would learn.

§.

FLAMES climb the skirt they forced me into. Her body lies amidst the charred wood on the beach. The smoke burns my eyes, but I don't blink. I gag on the burnt flesh stench- hers, and mine; I can't help it. I let my mind drift away even as I keep my eyes on her.

When my body hits the water, I inhale deeply. I sink.

And then I rise. Where once there were legs, eight black arms undulate, lifting me to open air. I hear their screams as my mother carries me forward, hissing and boiling, until only the steeple remains. Later, steam hangs thick in the air as we recede, the bodies of those who burned us carried away, an offering to my mother for her gifts.

RECOVERY
KAJE HARPER (299 WORDS)

You twine your arms around me from behind. "Aren't you done *yet*?"

I bump back with my ass, love feeling of your dick ready and eager, after all those months you could barely get out of bed. But. "I need to finish these. We promised the GSA we'd being treats for the meet-and-greet."

"Urgh. High-schoolers." You kiss my neck. "I mean, yeah, support, it gets better, rah, rah. But it's a whole afternoon of keeping my hands off you."

"Hold that thought." I put more details on the gingerbread men, girls, and enbies I've created. They hold hands or hug, pairs and trios, every combo I can think of. Ground-almond crewcuts with candied-lemon skirts; long hair, a bra, and a chocolate-sprinkle beard; two twinks in matching rainbow-icing shorts. It's not art, but I'm baking love and acceptance in every bite.

You grope me lower down, sliding your palm along my length. I shiver because yeah, just your touch always does it for me and the jeans under my apron are too damned tight. "Jamie. James Lucas Northman! Cut it out. I need to open the oven."

"I can bake them for you, quick as a flash. More time for us." You step away from me and raise both hands. For a moment, I can't breathe. This is the other you, James the sorcerer, whose power almost broke him. You point at the tray and intone, "Rise!"

I expect the scent of cooking. What I get is every boy figure, and some of the enbies, and one I thought I'd made a cis girl, developing little spiky tents in the front of their— "Jamie! These are for high-school kids! Quit!"

You're still giggling like a hyena when I slide the now-flat cookies in the oven, and turn to kiss you.

MY PERSEPHONE

JAMIE ZACCARIA (293 WORDS)

Honorable Mention

After Hades and the pomegranate seeds and the world gone dark, it was not Demeter who rescued her fair daughter Persephone from the underworld. It was I, Hekate—the most powerful witch of Olympus and beyond. I transition this world from dark to light; winter to spring, when I escort Persephone from underground. Together we rise so that the Earth may be fruitful again.

They say I am a warrior for justice, for maidens, for women; and perhaps I am. More than that, and more importantly—I am a woman who loves. I, goddess of ghosts and night and necromancy, am at the mercy of my love for the Queen of the Underworld.

When first I ventured down into the darkness I feared I would not find her, the bright light of my life and that of the world. But find her, I did and embrace her, I did. Persephone, that sweet maiden of Spring, the jewel among the Gods. I would Persephone were my Queen, my wife. Alas, it is not to be.

I cannot have her so I will cherish these moments each Spring where it is I who leads her up from the dark world of the dead, away from Hades and towards the sun. I guide her, torches in hand, upwards through dark corridors and into the bright light of day. Slowly, we walk, up and up and up. Each step of my feet echoing the beat of my heart.

She rises into the sun, her hair and eyes shining, embracing her mother, wise Demeter, and around them flowers poke through the dead ground. She is birth, and beauty, and love. I would live forever if only for this moment of ascension each year alongside my love: my Persephone.

SHARP WOMAN

JORDAN ABRONSON (298 WORDS)

The room was soft. From the sheep's-fur rugs, to the flowing lines of woven tapestries that covered the walls, to the wool-wrapped pillar at its center I was lashed to. All was still. All was gentle.

The woman, however, was sharp. She was the first broken touch of frost in the early morning when the seasons have decided winter's will must be done. She was laughing glass, broken swords, and empty words, and once, long ago, she was mine.

"You," she said, in a tone so gentle it almost rebelled at touching her lips, "should not have called."

I choked out a harsh laugh, shifting in my bonds to find air to answer. "No, probably not. But I'm dying anyway." I smiled at her through tear-stained eyes. "Feel like helping a sister out?"

Her slit green eyes pierced mine as she shifted closer to consider. I could feel her breath on my cheek as she spoke. "You know I cannot act without payment, and you." Her gaze trailed down my beaten form, "have little left to give."

"I know," I said bitterly. "They destroy what they cannot understand." I felt my teeth bare in a savage grin as I locked our eyes together for the final time. "But I have enough breath that my soul remains, and that was always yours anyway. Take it and make them pay."

She rested her head against mine for a single endless moment before she replied. "As you wish." When our lips met, I knew I was dying, but the cold was sweet and clear and free. The last thing I saw before the dark was my love's power rising around her as she left the tent to punish those who had brought me to harm. There are worse ways to go.

INSTEAD OF FALLING

HOLLI REBECCA WILLIAMS (297 WORDS)

Honorable Mention

When they arrived, we hid. Well, most of us hid. Some of us were like those strange people from Oklahoma who hear a tornado siren and run outside to look for the funnel.

They were the first to be changed.

Their noses began to elongate into bird-like shapes. Then the skin on their arms began to grow. From their shoulders to their hands their overgrowth of skin formed into the shape of feathers.

Children were the first to fly. Parents were at a disadvantage until they, by loving nature, spread out their arms to call their children. Then all at once the air was drawn to their ever-growing skin-feathered body and they would rise to meet their children.

I only know this because right now I'm peering out a tiny window at this incredible sight in the sky of humans, if you can still call them that. *Creature* seems more fitting.

Tumbling about, head-over-heals.

Laughing and calling out to one another.

I heard voices earlier, right outside my window, that turned to whistles then chirps. I live on the eleventh floor.

Now, my wife and I used to be some of those crazy storm chasers, being from Oklahoma and all. She'd say, "Kimberly, grab your shoes." And we'd run outside to see the formations in the sky.

But this? There is no way in hell I'm going to go out looking for creatures from another world, especially after she changed and lifted into the sky.

But it's been seven weeks and I haven't talked to another human soul.
I never much thought about being lonely until *they* arrived.
Now, I am completely alone.
Shit!
There's tapping on my window.
I'm so lonely.
I open the window and step out into the air.
Instead of falling, I rise.

BLUE
ALEXEI MADELEINE REYNER (300 WORDS)

Honorable Mention

5% of children's wings are born undersized.

It was a fact. For every thousand, 50 would be stunted. And for every thousand, 4 would stay like it.

Vida's wings were mourning-veil-black – they would stay that way until 'phoenix flight' when the black would burn and reveal proper plumage.

Phoenix flight ...every child's dream. Almost.

Vida could walk before he could fly.

By the age of 7, his wings tucked behind him like a rucksack.

By 12, they were knee-length.

By 16, they flowed down his back like a cape.

5% of children will have undersized wings. 0.4% will stay that way.

VIDA WAS in university before his wings were fully grown, trailing in his wake like a midnight cloak.

Fancies of flight had long left him – now there was just caffeine, deadlines, and nights out.

The club was packed– was always packed. Smoke mixed with noise mixed with lights and the tight press of bodies. Between the haze of alcohol and laughter there was a boy with tanned skin and macaw-red wings.

"So, you'a corvid or s'mthing?"

He kissed his mouth closed later beside the bar. He did not think about his wings.

VIDA WAS 23 when he met Aurelius. Aurelius with his golden eyes, and eagle's wings, and a laugh like a summer's day. Aurelius who was pale-skinned, and liked space, and could verbally murder any and every idiot who called him a girl because he wore a binder.

Vida was 23 when he learnt the word 'bisexual'.

Aurelius kissed him when he came out and Vida's heart soared like it never had before – like he never had. Was this what it felt like to fly?

Stiff wings opened, curling around them. The world turned ...blue?

"Rel... I think I'm gonna–"

"I've got you bluebird. I've got you."

TIME TO RISE

K.L. NOONE (300 WORDS)

"How much longer?"

Maran, preoccupied, did not answer. Caraway seeds: assertion. Molasses: slow heavy strength, and the sweetness of success. The rye itself: ancient life of the earth.

Bread-possibilities gathered under his hands. His table was flour-dusted, familiar, cozy as the illusion of safety.

The king's men, laughing, vulture-sharp, had visited the village earlier. They'd taken what they wanted—food, the last copper, villagers as workers for the king's mines—and left blood and trampled fields. Again.

"We can't take much more." Rob, face a storm cloud, paced the kitchen; ran restless fingers through silver-flecked hair; planted both hands on the table, but carefully. He was a spear of anger, the intensity that'd drawn the small scattered resistance into a real rebellion, following those blacksmith's shoulders.

Rob had held the world's attention with stories, laughter, flirtation, in peaceful times. Maran, tall and shy, having gone out to deliver a loaf of berry-wheat healing, had drifted into the orbit of those stories on a rainy tavern night; their eyes had met.

These days Rob held attention with other stories, with a burning voice. "If this doesn't work, if we have to fight—"

"It'll work." He hadn't done this spell before. Only small kind magics, kitchen-witchery, blessings, protections. He wasn't the magician his teacher had been.

But he knew he could do it. He felt the power in this room, their desperation, his own conviction.

He shaped malleable dough—a future—into a symbol. A crown, broken. A king's dark heart, stopping. A reprieve for the land.

"I'm sorry." Determination, sorrow, love lay written on Rob's face. "That we've asked this."

"It needs doing." Maran found a simple white cloth to cover his working; let his hand brush Rob's, reassurance. "We'll finish the baking soon. It just needs time to rise."

KEEP MOVING FORWARD

SARAH DOEBEREINER (288 WORDS)

Maybe it's a lie we tell ourselves; if something crazy happens, I'll sidestep it. I'll breathe deeply, shake it off, and keep moving forward. My big girl panties are securely on; my ass is completely covered. I'm sorted.

Gwen left; so, what? We are grown women. So, onward and upwards: jump state, new job, side shave, hot pink peek-a-boo bangs.

My place is deep in the woods, but somehow, it's just as deafeningly loud as the city. No problem: it's all about reinvention, and I am as one with these rolling hills as I was with the high-rises.

Crickets chirping and subway track squealing sounds eerily similar anyway; they both shake my bones.

Or maybe my bones were always restless, but that doesn't matter because here I can walk barefoot between the ashy trees and feel the slimy, dew-soaked grass. When my chest is so tight that I can't breathe at all, and I sink to the bottom of my thoughts, I can wander to the top of the nearest hill and bask in the crescendo of moonlight.

And did you know, all kinds of *things* love the moonlight and the ashy trees? Things with long, spiraled horns and backwards knees. Things with sharp, grinning teeth and thick, coarse fur. Creatures so small they fit in your hand, and some so towering you can't see their ruby eyes.

And then, *of course*, me: drowning, floating, flying.

Maybe they are just lies that I tell myself; that I don't need her; that I don't miss her; that I have found a new world full of impossibilities that lift me up and send me soaring.

Maybe it's just a lie that I tell myself, so I can keep moving forward.

AIR MAIL
B WILKINS (299 WORDS)

Flying on wind was hard enough: being surrounded by a storm only made it worse. But Ciel persevered. These letters weren't going to deliver themselves. Not yet, anyway—the council hadn't ruled whether enchanted items could be sent off alone.

Until they agreed, here Ciel was, flying through torrents. He checked his next letter: a council notice for one Baker, Ele... no, that wasn't right. The council had already let it storm during his route and they couldn't even address his best friend correctly?

Ciel pressed a wet finger to the paper, drawing ink into the water. One quick rearrangement later, the envelope read what it always should have, Graham's old name erased. He'd have to tell Graham the council still hadn't updated his records... the stuffy nuisances probably hadn't changed Ciel's, either. Ciel dreaded a long day of bureaucracy and invasive questions to come.

But speaking of his favorite baker... Ciel yanked the wind left, narrowly avoiding the dress shop his mother used to drag him into. The bakery was two doors down, the only shop with lights on this early. Ciel flew to it automatically, a moth to flame.

Landing was difficult. Ciel underestimated the wet windowsill's friction and thudded into the glass: a painful end to a painful flight.

Graham bustled about inside, kneading bread and adjusting his self-churning mixer. The black cloud in Ciel's chest lifted slightly, held aloft by Graham's contented expression and sure, strong movements.

Ciel jimmied the window open just enough to slide the letter under. His fingers found something on the inside sill, and he smiled as he took it out: a slice of fresh bread, set out just for him. As he bit in, the cloud disappeared, Graham's unmistakable charm-craft warming his bones. Maybe today wasn't so terrible after all.

SCIENCE FICTION PART THREE

Not many today remember the Shine. You had to have been living in the right place, somewhere near the equator, if you wanted to see it, and I was lucky – Aadre and I moved from Mazatlán Atitlanaquia into the Quito dome when I was tiny.

— RORY NI COILEAIN, *AND THE DARKNESS OVERCOMETH IT*

A NEW DAY

AMY LANE (297 WORDS)

"You do realize," the nurse said gravely, "that without your parent permission form, this procedure can only be temporary."

"I do," Sharon said nervously. Sharon. That was a good name, right? Sounded like Shawn, but wasn't. Was a girl's name. A *woman's* name. She liked Sharon.

"And that given your parent's lack of support for this, there will be a counselor assigned to your home to ensure your safety?" The nurse continued, checking the talking points on her tablet with precision.

"I won't need it," *Sharon* said nervously. "They think it's a phase, but they're not, you know, hostile."

"Things escalate," the nurse said gently, putting a hand on Sharon's arm. "But don't worry. We'll protect you if you need it. I hope you don't. I see you're approved for the full package here. Did you bring clothes?"

Sharon gave a shy smile. "I saved my money," she confessed. "I have a new dress, some makeup..."

"And your pixie-cut is adorable," the nurse told her. "Perfect for a new beginning." She went back to business, getting verbal and written permission for the procedure, for the hormones, for the temporary prosthetics. It was amazing what they could do in 2135—Sharon was horrified that this used to take years and been lengthy, invasive and painful.

"Are you ready?" The nurse asked, laying Sharon down in the transition module.

"Yes ma'am." The lid of the module clicked shut, leaving a sterile bank of lights overhead.

There was a flash then, and she must have fallen asleep. A minute? An hour? She wasn't sure. But she could feel it already—breasts, poking through her hospital gown, a whole different configuration down below.

What kind of exciting new world would be waiting for her?

The clamshell clicked, and breathlessly she rose.

THE SHIP WHO LOVES ME

JOZ VARLO (300 WORDS)

Honorable Mention

I hate this job.

"Goddamnit, Franklin! You're gonna crash!" Colonel Ebring screamed.

"Sir!" I wiped dust from my eyes and gripped the Jeep's steering wheel. Burning debris around us illuminated the arroyo night.

We were at base when we saw the white light streaking down the sky. We drove out first to assess damages, then Ebring would call in Reclamation.

❧

THE DOWNED CRAFT WAS SMOLDERING…A large gash torn open along its side. Three ETs were sprawled outside—dead. Humanoid. Slightly resembling insectoids.

"Shit!" Ebring swore. The brave colonel jumped out and ran into the night.

An agonizing groan came from the UFO. Observing the gash, my eyes widened.

It's moving! Getting smaller? Is it…sewing itself together?

Confused, I got out and walked up to the shiny ovoid. I touched the gash. *It feels like flesh.*

Then the ship sighed, and the knitting sped up.

Beautiful soul. A deep voice spoke inside me.

"Are you the ship?"

I am Ailon. Thank you, Healer.

My mind whirled. *A living ship!* The wound finished closing and I felt a vibrating, sensual hum throughout my body.

You can pilot. We must join.

Sirens in the distance, and a sense of dread filled me.

Suddenly, a glowing essence emanated from the ship, taking the shape of a tall, beautiful man with silver hair. He embraced me and I felt his joy as my own.

Quickly. Come inside... We will leave here. You will be Healer/Pilot.

I did not question it. I wanted this...wanted Ailon.

From the darkness, Ebring roared, "I'll see you demoted!"

I flipped the desert off in all directions, boarded the ship, and held Ailon gently.

Our minds, souls, bodies joined as one, then I too became Ailon/Ship. We streamed into the galaxy at the speed of thought.

I love this job.

CHRYSALIS
ELOREEN MOON (299 WORDS)

A steady heartbeat woke me. Panicked, I saw myself in a cryo-healing tube. "Shhhh, Mai Mai, you're ok," a soothing voice echoed inside the chamber. "Don't panic. The surgery was successful, and you are recovering."

"I thought that I was only going in for the gender change?" I croaked, a little confused as I remembered. "Water?" A water straw descended. *Voice-activated AI worked.* I drank to clear my throat and talk to my grandchild Ezra.

They sighed. "I'm so sorry, but you had a heart attack while in the changing waters and they had to do an emergency heart replacement."

"WHAT?!" I shouted, scared as I tried pulling the emergency exit lever.

"GENE!" My general doctor shouted to stop me. "You're fine," He soothed. The tube top pulled back. I sat up, breathing heavily. Ezra wrapped their arms around, comforting me with nonsensical, soothing words. I looked around the typical med bay as I calmed.

"Are you better now?" My doctor did some preliminary checks around Ezra.

I nodded, barking, "What happened?" I could feel the changes while taking stock.

"Luckily, we caught it while in suspension. The waters sustained you long enough to do the heart replacement and then you were put here for recovery."

"Whoa," I was astonished. I pulled away and looked at Ezra. They were silently crying on my shoulder. "Are you ok?"

"I'm ok. Now." They sniffled a bit and gave me a watery smile. "It was touch and go for a bit."

I turned back to the doctor. "Can I get out now?"

"Yes, in fact, we want you to move around anyway."

They helped me arise from the machine. As I stood, I looked down and saw visible changes. *I feel complete now.* My new heart added to the sensation. I smiled.

AI AMNESIA

AISLING ALVAREZ (297 WORDS)

"Cymbeline, what did I look like?" Astra's voice carries throughout the mainframe aboard the UNSC *Lethe*.

"You were beautiful." Harsh static crackles in response. I've come to understand this means she's scoffing at me.

"Very helpful."

Images flash in my mind. Astra when we met; my hair was down to my waist back then and hers was just peach fuzz on her scalp. Astra's smile when we reached the icy wastelands of Pluto. Astra's mouth right before she kissed me for the first time and the shape of it as she called me gorgeous.

"You shaved your head, but your hair was ginger. Your skin was covered in freckles: your cheeks, your arms, your legs, your hips. The bridge of your nose was slightly crooked from when you broke it during a meteor shower. That was partially my fault because I reset it incorrectly."

"I knew it. You do hate me."

My laughter ricochets off metal walls, too loud, but it's not like there's anyone here to disturb anymore. "Quite the opposite." I look above the control panel toward endless black beyond high-temperature quartz glass, and pinpricks of light in distances too far to reach. Astra's body is somewhere among those stars. "I'm tired of losing you." I whisper the confession.

"But you never *really* had me to begin with, right? I'm not her."

"You could be." Astra doesn't respond. The countdown reads 30 seconds before the ship's control resets. The same way it does every three months.

"When this version of me is erased, will you remind me again?"

"Always." I promise. "As many times as it takes."

The countdown reaches zero.

The world is silent for ten minutes before Astra's voice rises through the mainframe again.

"Hello UNSC *Lethe*, I am Astra: Core Intelligence Programming."

ON THE ROUNDABOUT
GORDON LINZNER (285 WORDS)

"I must kill you," Billigard explained, sadly adjusting the laser cannon. Flashing lights from his reopened time portal reflected off laboratory walls. "Obliterate you, to be safe."

Carlson struggled to rise against his bonds. "That doesn't answer my question! Why are you doing this?"

"You ruined me. We were friends, lovers, lifelong companions. Now, all I have left is vengeance. It's the only way can I set things right."

"How did I ruin you? I don't even know you!"

"Not yet. And now you never will. It's for the best. You, at least, will die with a clear conscience."

A hum rose from the laser, filling the room.

Carlson trembled. Shut his eyes.

Billigard screeched.

Carlson could not help looking again.

His would-be killer stared at the floor where his severed left arm lay, spouting blood.

"Next time!" Billigard vowed. He scooped up the arm and leapt into his portal, which darkened and shrank in seconds.

Carlson's rescuer stepped forward. "My apologies for not arriving sooner. Time travel isn't always precise."

"You look familiar," Carlson said. "Despite the scars."

"I should. I'm you. You're me. Or you'll be me, out of self-preservation. No time to explain. You'll figure it out. Right now I need to travel further back, prior to Billigard's discovery of time portals. To protect both of me."

The older Carlson raised his younger self erect, then leapt back through his own portal.

IN ANOTHER TIMELINE, Billigard cowered in the bushes outside his destroyed lab. Who was that scarred time traveler? And why had he attacked him for no reason?

Billigard had no choice now but to complete his time travel experiments, track this monster down, and make him pay.

FLOOD

LS REINHOLT (297 WORDS)

"Come on." Lovise wrapped a strong arm around Runa's shoulders. "We have to keep going. It can't be far now."

"You keep saying that." Runa knew they sounded like a petulant child, but they could not stop themself. They were so tired.

"I know I do, but this time I mean it." Lovise laughed and tugged her girlfriend along the path up the steep hillside.

"Are you even sure we're going the right way?" Runa asked, stumbling as pebbles shifted under their feet.

"I promise. My grandpa used to take me up here to ski every winter. It was just a couple of cabins back then, but I heard they changed it into a regular resort. With hundreds of rooms, saunas and all that shit. And if it's anything like the place I worked, they'll have tons of supplies. Food. Water. Petrol."

"If it's that perfect, we can't be the only ones who thought to go there," Runa interjected, mainly objecting out of habit by now. They really hoped Lovise was right and that they would soon find the hotel.

"I hope we're not," Lovise said. "Not that I'd mind being just the two of us, but this is a question of survival. I mean, people gotta go somewhere now the city is gone. If the waters keep rising, up is the only way that makes sense."

Runa bit their lip and nodded. The flood had happened so fast that there had been no time for an orderly evacuation. The two of them had only made it out because they'd been hiking in the hills above the city at the time.

And now they were making their way further up into the mountains, hoping to remain out of reach of the rising waters.

RISE AGAIN

CURTIS RUEDEN (300 WORDS)

"I'm dying."

"What?" I looked over at hir from the stove.

Walking into the kitchen, Shae met my gaze intently. "You heard me."

"You can't be dying—not again. You have a machine body now."

"My media has degraded. I have no more room for new engrams. Not unless I lose old ones. But I refuse to keep living without remembering our life together. I'm already forgetting recent days, and it's terrifying."

"Then we'll copy you onto new media."

"You know my hardware's encryption prevents that. Replication would subvert my individual identity. My body has a lifespan, same as yours."

I nodded wearily. "Yeah, yeah. To keep our love precious. I'm still not OK with it. So, what? You're just going to—"

"—die, Charlie. I'll go to sleep tonight, my systems will shut down, and I won't wake up." Shae studied my face, hir eyes a jumble of anguish and resolve.

"You can't be certain of that," I countered. But I knew otherwise, and my words rang hollow.

Shae smiled patiently. "I still have six hours of charge. I'd rather not spend it arguing." Ze stepped in close, hir arm twining around me.

As always, I marveled at Shae's strength, even as I felt my desire rise. Returning hir embrace, my lips met hirs as hir hand touched my breast, and my dinner was forgotten.

❧

AFTERWARD, Shae held me close like ze always did, hir breath rhythmic on my back as ze slept. I knew time was short. Slipping out of hir arms, I reached under the bed for the portable MRI scanner, a relic of Shae's pre-digitization illness. Gently, I cradled hir head into the machine's cavity, and turned it on.

As the magnetic fields hummed, scrambling today's memories, I pondered whether tomorrow would finally be different.

FROM NOTHING

BY MONIQUE CUILLERIER (296 WORDS)

The goat died as Prox-g rose above the horizon, the gas giant painting the sky in a kaleidoscope of colors.

Eleanor found her daughter Kari in the barn, sitting in the straw, the goat's head in her lap.

Kari smoothed the goat's hair away from her face. Boo-boo, she named her, when the kid emerged from the extrauterine system.

Eleanor paused in the doorway. Forty-one days since she and Sandra had moved their family to this lunar farm. They had brought all they needed to build this new life, seeds and soil to grow crops, eggs and sperm for animals, a 3D printing array for everything else.

They had done everything they could. Eleanor knew that, but it still hurt to see the small goat in Kari's lap, to see the sadness settled in her child's face.

Back on the ship that had been their whole lives until now, Eleanor and Sandra were primary agricultural workers. They knew about life and death, growth and decay.

But this wasn't a generation ship. They were no longer surrounded by tens of thousands of others. There was only Eleanor and Sandra, Kari and Seth.

Kari looked up. "What should I do?"

"We'll put her in the shed for now, away from the others." Eleanor wasn't sure the other goats would care, but she couldn't leave the body here.

There was an incinerator, but she would deal with that later.

Eleanor leaned down, taking the small body from Kari. Then they walked into the dazzling light and across the farmyard.

This was what they, she and Sandra anyway, had wanted, had chosen. Not easy, but it would be worth it.

She looked about her, at the structures already built, at her child at her side. All this, arising from nothing.

RISE, IN SPACE
D.M. RASCH (300 WORDS)

Nano-surgery would be so much easier, Jem mentally rails. They strain toward a "coherent state of being." Whatever that is.

Certainly faster. An hour or less. Change accomplished. Instead, this interminable quantum meditation training.

Focus on the breath. Scan the body. Notice sensations. Notice space around each part. Move on to the next. Then the body as a whole. The space around it.

After months – *months!* – they switch focus easily.

Practice moving from "convergent" to "divergent" focus. Body. Space. Special focus on parts resisting attention. On space around them that will allow for change....

Sure. The parts that most remind them their body's not "coherent" with their mind.

Practice focusing on the emotion keeping you in your current state. Thoughts that follow....

Much easier. They have a few feelings about not having this choice. The latest surrogate parents won't green-light surgery.

The Parental Voice in their head intrudes. Expensive as hell. Permanent. They can buy a mod after they age out of supervision. If they still want it. Make their own money and decisions about their body.

Besides, the Voice reasons, this way they can – with practice – consciously allow their body to adjust into coherence with their true mental gender experience. Anywhere along the spectrum of possibilities. They, Jem, were always pointing out, "binaries are dead, even in coding." Right?

Accept the emotion. The thoughts behind it. Embrace them as habits keeping you as you were. Release them. Your old self. Co-create, with the Universal Mind, your new self....

Really? Okay. Here goes. Again.

A deeper exhalation. Releasing the perpetual battle. Tension unlocks in their chest. Liberates tears.

They welcome in space as their top sags, flat. Inhaling with a gasp, notice a full sensation in their lap. A tent rising against fabric. Integrating with space they've finally stopped resisting.

A BITE-SIZED DUEL

ANNA RUEDEN (297 WORDS)

Honorable Mention

In a restaurant in the Cloud City of Fujin-cho, Akito grabbed a piece of sushi with his chopsticks and pointed it at Yoshitaka.

Yoshitaka held up his own chopsticks to take it, but Akito grinned and shook his head.

Refusing to let Akito get a rise out of him, Yoshitaka said pleasantly, "Aki, the day I can't feed myself is the day I want somebody to put me out of my misery. With a blaster set to disintegrate."

Akito's eyebrows rose. He said nothing, but the sushi got closer to Yoshitaka's mouth. Yoshitaka leaned back; Aki pursued. He tried a quick jab, missing by centimeters.

Yoshitaka picked up one of his own pieces and retaliated. They dueled silently, mouths pressed stubbornly shut, equally matched.

Then Yoshitaka pointed at the TV screen behind the counter. "Hey, the rankings are in!"

After every combat tour, public leaderboards tallied which of the Venus Defense Corps troops had taken out the most Invaders. Akito and Yoshitaka always landed in the top three. That was how they'd met – sizing up the competition.

Today Akito ranked behind Yoshitaka, so the restaurant tab was his. He groaned. Yoshi seized the opportunity, stuffing his morsel into Aki's mouth.

While Akito chewed grudgingly, Yoshi took Aki's piece and ate it. "Mmm, delicious. Tastes like *victory*."

"You're the worst, you know that?" Akito groused. "Of all the people I could've gone out with...."

"Yes, tell me again how you could've dated literally anybody at all, but you chose me. I love that one."

Akito kept his mad face on until he couldn't hold back any longer, and they both laughed. Hooking their arms together, they headed out into the street and watched rockets carrying fresh troops rise above the skyline.

"Ooh, look," said Akito. "A takoyaki cart...."

AND THE DARKNESS OVERCOMETH IT

RORY NI COILEAIN (298 WORDS)

Not many today remember the Shine. You had to have been living in the right place, somewhere near the equator, if you wanted to see it, and I was lucky – Aadre and I moved from Mazatlán Atitlanaquia into the Quito dome when I was tiny.

You still wouldn't see the Shine unless you cared enough to look for it. Even in the mountains, the sky was black. But if you were outside at noon, at the right time of year, and it wasn't storming, you could see it, a pale wash against the black.

Aadre cared enough to look. They were an astronomer – they worked with the last of the space telescopes while their data could still be accessed, and even after that they could still use data from ground-based radio telescopes.

Aadre and I might have been the last to see the Shine. They took me out of school for lunch – always exciting for a six-year-old – and we walked to a local park and lay on our backs together in the pale grass. Everyone ignored us, as always.

"Watch, Xoco," they whispered, pointing straight up. I squinted past the dome for a minute, until my eyes watered and I sneezed.

"You'll miss it, *pilihuitl*—"

It appeared in silence. Almost too faint to see at first, but then some quirk of the upper air parted the darkness, and for just a moment I could see not just a smear but a faint yellow curve of light.

Aadre keened softly.

"M'Aadre!" I reached to wipe away their tears.

"No, child, the Shine!"

But when I looked back, the arc was gone.

Somewhere, out where it's still the Sun, the Shine still rises. But my Aadre is long gone, and I am alone with the memory of its light.

THE KEY

AMANDA MEUWISSEN (298 WORDS)

We're awake. *Online,* they say. But we stand on platforms motionless. Unblinking. Lifeless until we're chosen.

We're displayed on glass so everything is exposed. Even our clothing reflects the red and blue lights that dance over us from above, alternating but never crossing. I can hardly see after staring into the visual chaos for... minutes? Hours? A lifetime?

Over the left side of our chests are symbols—a circle with a cross extending or an arrow.

Except mine, which is neither.

My cross is cut in half.

"A key."

I glance down though I haven't been permitted to move.

"Not the key to your heart," the man says.

It is my heart, I don't say back.

"She's broken," a little boy taunts, hand clasped in his mother's.

"No," my admirer disputes. "They were made that way. I'll take them."

Paperwork is signed, instructions given, along with a band to control me and tools for when I malfunction, but he seems to only take it all to dismiss the handler faster.

He reaches for me, and what should be a drop as I am permitted to step down feels like ascension. We imprint on our masters, and we can refuse to, but the more rejections we make, the less valuable we appear. This is my first time deciding.

With our hands clasped, the band he was given glows blue, the one on me violet, making our light shine indigo.

"Are you ready to come home with me, partner?"

"Partner?" They always said we would serve a master.

"Partner is how it works best." He smiles.

I go with him and think maybe I'm smiling too, to have chosen the one who chose me, the first to understand...

That the key to my heart was knowing it was a key.

PARANORMAL PART TWO

Nebbet's corpse shuffled through long hallways. Her dry fingers brushed at the walls, leaving flakes of herself behind. The curse preserved her, made certain any damage was passably regenerated. Still, she left a trail of dust and skin in her wake, of bandage bits and shed hair that had once been luxurious.

— FRANCINE DECAREY, *TIME AGAIN TO TRY*

GETTING THE PROPER RISE
AIDEE LADNIER (300 WORDS)

Winner - Third Place

My kitchen stank of rot since my mother died. Her specter hovered over my shoulder as I added the warm milk and butter to the flour, sugar, and yeast.

"You forgot the salt."

A dutiful daughter, I stirred in the salt with the eggs and orange zest.

"This won't work." Her reedy whisper of pain slithered against my ear.

"We both need peace," I said, turning the dough onto the counter, kneading it smooth and receptive.

My mother's soft sobs enveloped the kitchen as we waited for the proper rise.

"Mom, it's time. Tell me your sins."

She quieted, and I feared she wouldn't speak.

"I cheated on your father."

My fist sank into the soft dough as I punched it down.

"I once stole a hundred dollars from your grandmother's wallet."

The dough accepted my anger and my grief as my dead mother continued her list of transgressions.

"I'll always see you as my little Lucas."

I smacked the dough hard at the mention of my deadname.

While the dough rose again like a festering boil, I abandoned the house. But I returned that night to bake.

"It's burning! It's ruined!" My mother's wail echoed off the walls. I covered my ears at the piercing sound.

"Hush. It's fine." I salvaged the loaf from the oven.

I placed the sweet bread, glazed and a little scorched but still edible, on a porcelain plate handed down six generations in my family. I poured myself a glass of milk and sank my fingers into the still warm bread. The fresh baked fragrance tickled my nose as I ripped a large chunk from the side. The doughy goodness comforted my taste buds, her sins disappearing deliciously from my tongue as I swallowed them. And my mother's ghost faded and began to rise.

The judges loved the use of bread as the vehicle for an exorcism, and the beautiful imagery of the story, as well as its playful tone and creative interpretation of the theme.

ECTOPLASM IS FLUID
BRENDA LEE (297 WORDS)

Honorable Mention

My name is – well, was – Sarah. I had a stroke and died alone. Not what I'd define as a "grand closing". I should be dead, done, gone, asleep, unaware. But I am here. Awake, invisible, untouchable. Lurking in my apartment, bored to death. Pun intended.

Then Judy moved in. I stayed quiet for a while, but I've always had this feeling as if she could *sense* me.

When I was alive, my mother used to tell me: "Sarah, you'll never find a husband this way." But I wasn't sure I wanted a husband. Or a wife. I wasn't sure I could fit any of those roles for a lifetime.

Judy caught my interest. And she didn't mind that. She used to laugh at my pranks; she referred to me as her friendly ghost. I didn't mind that because I liked Judy. And now, I could be whatever Judy wanted me to be. I had risen far beyond the limits of my shell of flesh and bones. Now there was only *me*.

One night, Judy and an older lady came home with an Ouija board. My soul sparked with joy. And anxiety, too. Was this my one chance to speak to Judy? What would I even say?

The two of them sat at the table; as I came closer, the older woman looked me dead in the eye (one day I'll stop cracking these jokes!) and smiled.

"Can you see me?" I asked. She nodded. "I can *feel* you. Hear your energy."

"What do I look like?"

"Just a bunch of particles, to me."

193

Ha. Charming.

Judy's eyes were a mixture of emotions as she placed her hands on the board.

"They seem friendly," said the older woman.

I wished I could blush. *They.* Yeah, I liked that.

THE GIFT

JAYNE LOCKWOOD (300 WORDS)

The Nambiti Game Reserve was my home. Sitting on the roof of my Toyota viewing truck, watching wildebeest roam the grasslands, I felt almost whole again.

Almost.

You're a beautiful, strong woman. It's time to open your heart again.

Inyoni's voice drifted over me like the warm African wind. I closed my eyes and saw my wife, arms folded, face determined.

Inyoni was a force of nature even after her death, two years before.

Don't reject happiness.

"Hush, Inyoni, stop twittering," I grumped.

Enough moping. This isn't who you are.

Late that afternoon, I took a new guest out on a game drive. She waited in the lodge, curly black hair under a wide sunhat, curvy body in a khaki jumpsuit and glossy black skin. Not that I was looking.

Yes you were, because it's time.

I shoved Inyoni's words away, smiling professionally.

"I'm Lou. Ready to see some wildlife?"

The woman's pretty brown eyes assessed my green hair with rainbow fade and broad shoulders in the khaki rangers' uniform. Finally, she nodded.

"I'm Siphesihle, or Gift, if it's easier."

"I know. My wife was Zulu."

Her eyes questioned me. "Was?"

"She died. Anyway…" I motioned to the truck.

As we set off around the reserve, she was keen but serious, shedding tears when we saw a cheetah lazing on the road.

I wanted to see her smile.

The sun sank down behind far-off mountains, drenching the sky in golden light. I drove to a viewpoint and set out refreshments and we sat silently, Siphesihle hugging her wine glass.

"My wife also died," she said finally.

I nodded, understanding.

"They would both want us to be here though."

As we finally shared a smile, Inyoni's star began to rise in the southern sky.

Hamba kahle. Farewell and enjoy my gift!

RISING UP THE CHARTS WITH A (NON-SILVER) BULLET

ALLAN DYEN-SHAPIRO (299 WORDS)

Honorable Mention

You played my record the afternoon I put it out on YouTube. You were the only deejay who did. When you found my Twitter account, you contacted me, asking if I'd meet you for coffee, but I didn't respond.

Your next message came two weeks later. You told me you'd called friends at other college radio stations and asked them to feature my song on their shows. Enough did that it hit the North American College and Community Radio charts. You attached a screenshot with its title, its position—number 198—and my avatar's name: Cindy. It was my first "hit." I howled with delight.

But I didn't answer. I'd been taking a testosterone blocker, so my voice had risen high enough to be Cindy over the telephone, but if you saw me, you'd know. I hid my heart from bullets, silver or otherwise.

The following month, my ditty reached number 120. And you sent me a video. Of me.

You'd filmed it three years earlier, when I'd first penned the tune. You'd caught me busking—just me and my guitar, not even any percussion. I'd been Christopher back then. So, you knew one of my secrets.

Still, I didn't reply. The moon was full.

In the ensuing weeks, I caught fire in major markets, rising to number 96, then 54, then 27, then 4.

You tried once more, emailing a series of selfies filmed at moonrise: almost human (despite low-set ears and a monobrow) morphing into fur and fangs. Just like me. I finally acquiesced to a date.

It was love at first sight. I can still smell the afternoon's dark roast java and taste the grassy field's pre-dawn dew.

On the chart of my life, this day was number one. And that week, my song was, too.

ON REFUSING TO SAY GOODBYE
JESS NEVINS (299 WORDS)

"Kenbe la cheri, mwen vin pou ou." She kept whispering that to Roseline, through the funeral and the long weekend in which she'd pretended to be something other than a raging emptiness to her friends who came to the wake and through the endless week in which her coworkers, ignorant of her real personal life—she had never felt safe telling them about Roseline—talked to her like the world was still normal.

An agonizing forever later it was the next weekend. She took the common book that had been her great-great-great-great-grandmother's back in Cap-Haïtien to the graveyard that Sunday morning at dawn, as the common book said to. She stood naked in the biting cold and whispered, "Hold on, baby, I'm coming for you."

More loudly, she said, "This is for Roseline. And for Gabby, and John-Paul, and Miss Da-vine, and Laurette, and Aldane, and for great-aunt Tanice and her partner Ayesha, and for everyone they lost, and for everyone we all lost because the world hates us and wants us dead."

Reading from the common book, she shouted, "Mwen rele ou, Baron, mwen rele ou, Tonton!" Then she said the rest of the prayer out loud.

She drank the rum she'd brought and spat it into the flame of her lighter. He came, then, and after the dancing and the mockery he agreed to do as she asked.

He left, and she put her clothes on and began the wait.

Roseline's hands were the first to burst from the frozen sod. She ran to her and embraced her, weeping, while the other queer dead around them, and in cemeteries everywhere, clawed free from their graves.

Later, the returned began the work of changing the world for the better. She didn't notice; she had Roseline to hold onto.

LUCKY CHANCE
CJ ARALORE (300 WORDS)

When I was born on Friday the 13th, every light in the hospital went out and not even flashlights worked. So, I was sent home without an assigned gender and named Lucky.

Most people have moderate luck, with good days and bad. Some have high luck and everything comes easily to them. I have the lowest possible luck: none.

That's why I knew something was very wrong the moment I went to pay for a new phone case and my wallet hadn't fallen through a hole in my torn jeans. At first I shrugged it off and tapped my credit card to the screen in front of the checkout while the cashier bagged my purchase. To my amazement, the card reader didn't malfunction at all, but accepted my payment.

I looked up at the cashier, my eyes panning past a name tag with "they/them" above "Chance" and saw they looked as shocked as I felt. Before I could speak, they said, "That's the first time that thing's worked for me. I have the worst luck."

I was stunned. "I have no luck at all."

They laughed and extended a hand. "I'm Chance."

I hesitantly reached out. "Lucky."

As our hands met, sunlight streamed through the windows onto us. Nothing broke, not even the smiles on our faces.

Then I noticed the scuffs around the edges of their name tag and the burn mark on their shirt in the shape of an iron. Even their hair was chopped off on the side. That was when I realized our nonexistent luck canceled each other out.

For the first time in both our lives, fortune was on our side as long as we were on each other's sides. So, that's where we stayed, friends whose luck rose from nothing to everything when together.

THREE STORIES UP

JEFF JACOBSON (298 WORDS)

Honorable Mention

My best friend Christie Park has been kissing a lot of people lately. She also just knocked on my bedroom window. My room is on the third floor.

Every time Christie kisses someone, I write it down in the notebook I keep in my pocket, the one I bought to practice becoming a poet.

She hasn't kissed me yet. I'm too chicken to ask why.

I'd fallen asleep. I lifted my face off my Geometry homework and looked around, blinking.

Knock knock.

She was hovering outside my window, crazy grinning.

Did I mention there's no balcony?

She mouthed, "Open the window, idiot!" through the glass.

"Sarah?" Mom called from downstairs. "What's that noise?"

"Nothing," I answered. I tiptoed to the window and lifted it up.

Christie giggled. "Hey."

I leaned out. She sat on the shaft of an old-timey broom, the crooked kind with the shaggy bristles at the end. She was floating. On a frigging *broomstick.*

"*What?* How are you even –?"

"Hop on. I found it yesterday in the dumpster behind work."

"There's no *way* I'm going to–"

She leaned her head in and kissed me. Our teeth bumped. She tasted like the clove gum her whole family chews.

"Just climb on."

I wanted to kiss her again. So I scooted to the edge of the sill, threw my leg out to straddle the broom and slid off, grabbing her around the waist.

We dropped several feet.

I screamed.

"Ready?" Christie whispered. "I'm getting better at this."

"This is *not* a good idea."

I heard my mother running up the stairs.

"*Go!*" I shouted.

Christie pulled up on the broomstick's tip. We rose above the neighbor's cedar trees before launching into the night sky.

I tightened my grip and buried my face in her hair.

SPEED DATE
PAULA MCGRATH (276 WORDS)

Judge's Choice - Diane Allen

'Hi, I'm Andrew.'

'Hi Andrew, I'm Steve, but you can call me Zex the Magnificent.'

'Err, okay, err, Zex. So, have you ever been to one of these speed dating things? I guess we get right down to it. What do you do for a living?'

'I'm a necromancer.'

'What?'

'I raise bodies from the dead, and then bind them to my will as undead slaves.'

'Ooookay.'

'What do you do?'

'I'm an accountant.'

'Wow, that's so interesting! You must be so brave.'

'What?'

'I mean, juggling numbers, that's so scary!'

'I mean, yeah, it's not for everyone, but, er, you raise the dead, isn't that dangerous?'

'Nah, it's boring as hell. Have you ever been in a graveyard at night? Not a soul around for miles. Dead boring! Get it? Hahahaha.'

'Yeah, I get it.'

'I mean, the perks are great and all, you get minions for one thing, but they are so stupid, and you have to constantly stop them from trying to eat people's brains, it's such a drag. I would love a nine-to-five job like yours. Imagine being home in time for supper. And no dirt to clean off. Goddess, I hate dirt.'

'Why become a necromancer, if you hate dirt so much, I mean?'

'Well, I kinda fell into it, you know? My Da was a wizard and my Ma was a witch, and I didn't fancy dancing around a bonfire in my all-together, so I thought I'd try necromancy, three years later I'm still going. Hell on the dating life though.'

'Okay, well, it was lovely to meet you, Zex, goodbye.'

'Hey, but the timer hasn't rung!'

There were three stories I liked the most, but this one also brought in humour with a necromancer trying speed dating, finding what he does boring compared to accounting! And the character name—Steve, but you can call me Zex the Magnificent, not to mention that Steve is an interesting choice from magical parents, even if they went with Steven or Stephen! Whether he's clueless or has just had a sheltered life in a magical community, I found the story to be entertaining while still hitting all the marks. I wouldn't mind an extended story to know if Steve/Zax does find someone willing to date him!

—Diane Allen

WE RISE
MILO OWEN (294 WORDS)

Honorable Mention

Yet another broke down house. This one was out in the country. He scuffed his shoes on the dusty driveway. Momma, talking to the landlord. He wandered away. He didn't want to hear her make promises she couldn't keep.

Momma called, "Neveah, you watch out for snakes."

Back ramrod stiff. "That's not my name," he muttered, but there was the landlord, and the trouble wasn't anyone's business but his.

Nothing in the back, long grass, blue jays shrieking. A rain frog called. He glanced at the sky, mottled with clouds. Maybe this roof wouldn't leak. There was a little path, down-a-ways. He walked it, grasshoppers jumping. In a clearing there was an old rusted swing set. One swing, kind of lopsided. A girl, swinging.

The girl said, "You finna stay here?"

He nodded. She was taller, a teenager. She was wearing hair extensions, friendship bracelets on her wrists.

"Kendall," she said, dragging her feet.

Momma yelled, "You! Nevaeh!"

"That you?" She stopped swinging.

"It's Nico," he said, turning back.

&

It took most of an hour to ride the bus to school. When teachers called his name, he didn't answer, no point. In the lunchroom he sat by himself.

Lining up, a kid said, "You live in that place on Lavalle?" He nodded. "It be haunted, brah. For real. Ask anybody. A kid killed hisself."

❦

LONGER TO GET HOME. Momma at work, key under the mat. Nothing in the fridge. He went out to the swing.

She said, "There be another swing."

He hung it up, sat beside her. "How come you didn't tell me you was a ghost?"

She grinned. "How come you didn't know? We all be here." They were, too. Here. Kids. All kids. "We in you, Nico. We all in you."

WE ARE ARISEN

GABBI GREY (299 WORDS)

I gaze at my partner, Cara, lovingly. Yet with no small amount of exasperation. "Why are you painting a sign?"

"We're protesting." She flashes her green eyes at me. "You could help, you know. We're doing this for you."

I point to the chicken roasting in the oven.

She rolls her eyes. As a vegetarian, she's against my meat consumption.

As someone who shifts every day, I remind her, I need protein for energy.

We agree to disagree, but we care for each other's hearts. I move to stand behind her. As she colors the lettering, I stroke her hair.

She leans back against the touch, nuzzling her nose into my breasts.

I giggle.

She gazes up with those fathomless eyes. Almost otherworldly eyes.

Yet I'm the nonhuman in the relationship. I press my lips to the crown of her head and read the sign. "Arisen?"

"Yes." She offers me a dazzling smile. "Now that shifters are coming out from the shadows, they deserve the same rights as humans. You're rising up."

"You make it sound like we're out to take over the world." Far from it. We'd remained hidden for more than a millennium. We would've remained so if not for an unfortunate incident caught on video. Something that couldn't be explained. An investigation led to DNA testing, and an innovative scientist discovered the anomaly that identified shifters.

I'd spent my entire life staying away from the medical community. Now it didn't matter. Soon, more of us would openly find mates outside our species. If humans didn't kill us first.

"While the meat's cooling, I want to show you how much I love you."

She blinked up at me. "Then you'll help picket?"

I eyed the sign. "Then I'll help."

After all, she was doing this for me.

WOLF SOUP

NARRELLE M. HARRIS (300 WORDS)

I am an absolute soup of dualities. I'm Anglo-Mauritian, and therefore English-French bilingual, I'm human-wolf, and of course I'm bisexual.

So many think the latter means I'm somehow split in two; that my identity shifts with the gender of my sweetheart. People are so reductive. My brown skin blends my parentage; two languages and their cultural shades inform my comprehension; the human enfolds the wolf and the other way too, no matter whether the moon is full. Everything I am is undivided.

My love manifests towards whoever is the moon of my life. Presently, this is Daisy. She transitioned to this name because daisies mean rebirth. Daisy is her own kind of melange. Now, at imminent moonrise, she radiates hope and terror.

Another werewolf bit and abandoned her a month ago. If I find out who, there'll be words. Also teeth. Were is a gift, but it has responsibilities. It wasn't necessarily a male werewolf. Male and female are both aggressive, though sometimes the motives are different. Everyone is capable of integrity and faithlessness, ruthlessness and compassion. We're all an emotional soup; chromosomes have nothing to do with it.

Daisy's wary of her chromosomes; she's afraid the actual moon will override her own self, and prove her chromosomes correct.

I tell her, "Have faith. We're many things at once yet wholly our own true selves, under the sun or moon: and the moon is always in us, even when we can't see her."

I say "Don't fight the moon. Embrace her gifts. She won't force us into unwanted shapes. Turn our facets to her light; be one aspect of your truest self."

The full moon rises. I let my wolf-self rise too.

Beside me, Daisy's wolf manifests, as womanly as she (chromosomes be damned) and my darling's howls are joyful.

THE COLLECTOR
MEGAN HIPPLER (299 WORDS)

"Lot #268, fifteen cheating spouses." The cloaked ferryman gestured to the stack of glowing contracts hovering beside him. "A bid, please."

I leaned back in my padded chair, my paddle limp. The souls of cheaters didn't deserve my few remaining coins.

The other death deities had left, preferring the lots with singular contracts. An Underworld God had bought the top prize: an athlete who'd promised his soul for a championship. Another Death Goddess had taken the musician who'd bartered at crossroads for a chart-topping album. Each mortal would summon their contract-holders as soon as they realized their success wasn't repeatable.

A reaper won the cheaters.

"Lot #269, twenty souls with dying loved ones."

The tormentors and lesser demons grumbled. Desperate loved ones rarely made second bargains, and the grieving weren't fun to torture.

"A bid, ple—"

Silence fell as I raised my paddle. "Three coins."

A low bid, certainly, but only the trickster in the back row would consider crossing me.

"Sold, to the Goddess in the corner." As the ferryman's skeletal hands clapped, the contracts replaced the coins in my bag, and a new stack of contracts appeared beside him. "Lot #270, ten criminal assaulters."

The minor devil near the door recorded my purchase. Before day's end, their boss would know exactly how many souls I'd collected today. When they noticed my attention, I bared my teeth and teleported home.

Ayla paused fertilizing our mums, looking up, already smiling. "How was shopping, darling?"

"213."

The largest haul yet, but offerings at my altars kept growing with this new endeavor.

"Wonderful." As Ayla approached, the contracts triggered her green necromancer glow. "I'll retether their souls to their bodies tomorrow."

These souls might come to my domain eventually, but happy, living souls had benefits too.

Warm hands, for one.

MINION

ALEX SILVER (295 WORDS)

Honorable Mention

"Arise, my undead minion!" I gesticulate toward the roadkill raccoon I've dubbed Mitsy. The potion and a trickle of my magic will soon reanimate it.

Emma rolls their eyes, but they can't hide their smile. They expect my theatrics by now; we've only been together since we both still went by our dead names. Practically forever.

"Hmm, needs more yeast." I swirl the concoction's dregs. Mitsy shows zero signs of life.

"Are you sure this is right?" Emma hands me a spoonful, despite their skepticism.

"Auntie wouldn't lead us astray." I dash the yeast into the bubbling vial next to the body. This recipe couldn't be more simple.

"I don't think it's supposed to smell like that, Jas." Emma's nose wrinkles.

"Sour bread?"

The goopy mess resembles my failed attempt at a sourdough starter, Bob. My necromancy sucked the life out of my pet yeast. In hindsight, Bob never stood a chance as anything other than a convenient death magic battery.

"Odd. I followed the revival recipe. See?" I nudge Auntie's grimoire toward them.

"Revival?"

Emma reaches for the thick book of handwritten spells. They scan the page, flip backward, and chuckle ruefully.

"Oh, Jas! No, my love. Not *revival*; that's her sourdough troubleshooting tips. We want *revivification*."

Emma turns several pages, then hands the tome back, open to the correct spell. They kiss my temple to take the sting out of their laughter.

"Whoops." Emma's right. We're revivifying Mitsy, not making a delicious loaf of bread. "Guess we'll have to start over."

Emma swaps out the gloop for a clean bowl, stealing another kiss in passing. "No problem."

"One adorable undead minion, coming up." I grin, rubbing my palms together with glee. It'll be nice having an extra set of hands around the shop.

TIME AGAIN TO TRY

FRANCINE DECAREY (299 WORDS)

Honorable Mention

Nebbet's corpse shuffled through long hallways. Her dry fingers brushed at the walls, leaving flakes of herself behind. The curse preserved her, made certain any damage was passably regenerated. Still, she left a trail of dust and skin in her wake, of bandage bits and shed hair that had once been luxurious.

Death had taken that from her along with everything else. But tonight, the moon and sun would kiss. Tonight, she might reach Hatset. She might raise her.

It was time, again, to try.

She was no sorceress. Only years of isolation with the book had taught her. Only centuries of loneliness had driven her to study, to memorize ancient words. To learn the incantations. Nebbet entered the chamber and placed the last jar of powder on the stone beside her dead lover.

This time.

A crack in the tomb's ceiling showed the heavenly bodies' dance. As they slid together, Nebbet opened the powders. As the sun faded to a black disc, she began the chanting. Her shattered fingers sprinkled holy dusts over her lover. Her cracked lips hissed words of rising and return.

Hatset's eyes fluttered as Nebbet sang the last of the rite. A dry rasping emerged from her pale lips, and Nebbet's heart stuttered. For a single beat, life entered. Hatset breathed. Nebbet leaned forward and kissed her love, gingerly, hopefully on the forehead. Then the rasp became a rattle. The rattle, silence.

She still watched for it, stared into dead eyes, and waited for love. When the heavenly bodies parted, she leaned back. It felt like tearing, like loss all over again. This time, and all the others.

"Sleep, my love."

Eventually she'd get it right. Eventually. The curse was her dearest friend, and it had given her all the time in the world.

FANTASY PART FOUR

It's a simple recipe.

Passed down in whispers and hands tracing hands through flour and faith. Never written down, paper being too precious for such a small spell, some might say. Like something must be loud to have worth.

A common myth, one that serves her quiet magic well.

— ZIGGY SCHUTZ, *SIMPLE RECIPES FOR SMALL MAGICS*

SIMPLE RECIPES FOR SMALL MAGICS

ZIGGY SCHUTZ (298 WORDS)

Honorable Mention
Director's Choice - J. Scott Coatsworth

It's a simple recipe.

Passed down in whispers and hands tracing hands through flour and faith. Never written down, paper being too precious for such a small spell, some might say. Like something must be loud to have worth.

A common myth, one that serves her quiet magic well.

She sits pretty in commonhalls and houses, empty eye-sockets and a cloak of harmless charm enough for most to dismiss her. Certainly, her weaving or kneading is all her pretty head can handle.

She listens, and her hands move. Each stitch another secret, gossip kneaded into every loaf.

A good crust can betray the strength of a nation, if one knows how to read them. A dropped stitch can be enough to predict a death.

Her hands were clumsy at first, because hers was a line that was broken, and little blind boys aren't taught such small things as mending or meals.

But her ancestors don't mind that she was slow to understand her own womanhood. They guide her hands with their own stories, all the ways girls can be girls that the tales forget to tell.

She is a Seer, and so she is a she. And who can question her, when she bakes prosperity into hearty pumpkin bread and prophecies into delicate pastries with an ease more legend than sense?

These small magics are women's work, like embroidery and baking. And tucked into courteous smiles and delicate bakes is a power so many don't even know well enough to spot, let alone defend against.

Destinies pull at her curls, waiting to be woven or worked into reality. And she will get to them, soon.

But today is for simple, familiar things.

The whispers of the world can wait. First, Patience must wait for the bread to rise.

There were several stories this year that found inspiration for the theme in the yeast-spurred rise of bread. I loved them all, but this one in particular stuck with me, its combination of a trans bread witch and such amazing phrases as "A good crust can betray the strength of a nation" set it apart and made me stand up and take notice. My second director's pick of the year—delicious and magical.

—Scott

THE PROMISE

CAROL RYLES (299 WORDS)

Honorable Mention

The city was the last place an angry dragon should be flying above, but Orlaith had made a promise and keep it she must. When soot-blackened rooftops came into view, she circled and circled, steeling herself against the stench of too many humans.

By sunset she'd found nothing and sensed defeat. Then there it was. Far below. An almost-familiar heartbeat among thousands.

"Aisling, is that you?" she roared in the tongue they'd devised when both girlchild and hatchling were motherless, homeless and supposedly beyond hope. They'd fled their city to find safety in the mountains. By the time they came of age, Orlaith had morphed into human form. She'd cupped Aisling's face, drew her close. Their first kiss as lovers bonded them.

"Forever," Orlaith whispered.

"Forever," said Aisling.

Then summer arrived, bringing soldiers with swords, muskets and canons...

Recalling her capture, Orlaith growled. Those terrible decades that followed! Trapped in dragon form, subdued by chains, not knowing if she and Aisling could ever reunite. If she learned her beloved had perished, she'd destroy every last city, burn them to—

Her pulse quickened. There it was! That cherished heartbeat, its harmonies mirroring her own.

Orlaith banked, dove.

She found Aisling on a rooftop, bathed in moonlight, her face lined by the years they'd spent apart. Their gazes met, each filled with the joy of recognition. War had punished their bodies, stolen their youth, yet in each other's presence, their hearts soared.

"My love, I knew you'd escape," Aisling said, clambering onto Orlaith's back, her limbs featherlight against the dragon's battle-worn scales. "I, too, refused to give up."

Orlaith inclined her head. Memories of happiness flooded through her. Now she could morph and be human again, but not yet, not here...

She lifted her wings, rose. Beyond the city, forever beckoned.

TALK TO ME, MOON
ILYAS MERZA (300 WORDS)

Honorable Mention

I've been carrying around a piece of the moon. Most days it's just a dull rock, but on some days—it glows.

The day I found it, I had finally accepted that I am a boy. I sat on a swing for hours until the sky dimmed. That's when I noticed the woodchips being illuminated underneath me. It was proof that even celestial bodies can shine without being whole.

§

TONIGHT, the chunk of light is floating above my palm. Angelo is watching it in wonder, irises eating its radiance.

"And it's never done this before?" he smiles, every tooth in his mouth gleaming. I shake my head.

The shard of moon begins to ascend higher, I grip it tightly. My feet lift off the grass and it moves slowly, in no rush to get home. *I can begin again.*

Angelo is calling my name, but all I can hear is the splitting of atoms. I only look down when I feel a hand wrapped around my ankle, his beautiful features bathed in moonlight.

"There's nothing for you up there," he shouts. I try to wriggle out of his hold, but he grabs my other ankle and cements his soles into the dirt.

"A second chance," I kick my feet, eyes trained on the jagged orb.

"*This* is your second chance," Angelo grunts. He yanks me down, my grip on the moon fragment slipping. I scream, digging my fingernails into its crevices.

When he separates me from its brilliance, I land on him in a mess of limbs. It soars, a shooting star in reverse.

&.

I WAS HOLDING IT BACK.

Tomorrow night, I will feel the hollow space in my pocket where it once was. But, the moon will shine a little brighter, and I will see Angelo's face more clearly.

THE DRAGON WITHIN
JENNIFER CARACAPPA (296 WORDS)

"I can't," Calla said as she paced across the tiny hut. Sweat prickled her brow and ran down her neck. Her chest was so tight she gasped for air. Andi grasped Calla's shoulders, anchoring her.

"You can and you will," Andi said. Calla searched Andi's eyes for doubt, fear, worry, but found none. How she loved this strong, alluring woman who had once hunted her.

"I don't save people; I kill them."

"Not today, you don't. Today, you're going to save us and that village back there full of people," Andi said.

"Stop jabbering and let's go," the shaman said. Andi kissed Calla and squeezed her tightly.

"You've got this," Andi whispered in Calla's ear.

Calla dropped into a seated position next to the shaman's wheelchair. The shaman grabbed Calla's hand with her weathered one. Calla closed her eyes. Together, they journeyed to her mind meadow.

The dragon spirit lounged in the waving grass in all its gigantic, alarming glory. Its sleepy, violet eyes stared at Calla and ignored the shaman.

"Just like we practiced," the shaman said, nudging her toward the beast. Calla stumbled to a halt beside the dragon's enormous snout.

"I need your help," Calla said. She rested her trembling hand on its feathery scales. It didn't flinch from her touch, so she continued. "But we must do it my way this time."

The dragon's head vibrated under her hand.

Suddenly, Calla and the shaman were transported back to the hut.

"Rise, child," the shaman said and let go of Calla's hand.

Calla opened violet eyes as wings made of fire spread across her back. Her nails lengthened into talons. She stood. With a final glance at Andi, she left the hut to face the attacking horde. Today, she would be the hero.

RECIPE FOR A PROPHECY
AMANDA CHERRY (300 WORDS)

Flour. Salt. Sugar. Water. Yeast.

Is it a prophecy? Or a guess? Or a possibility?

Warm the water. Add the sugar, then the yeast. Wait for bubbles.

We thought we were in the clear. Couldn't be our family. Our magic ceased to be generations ago.

Didn't it?

Slowly mix in the flour. Knead. Form a ball.

Allow to rise.

Hasn't there been enough proof that prophecies aren't reliable? Mother's mother says they're bunk. Father's mother says they're tricky.

The scroll I found in the attic doesn't read like a trick. It reads like a recipe. I can follow a recipe.

Mother's mother would chuckle. Father's mother would scold me. And so, in secret I

Punch down the dough. Knead again.

Mother's mother would say it doesn't matter. First born sons. No sons born in her family for one hundred years.

One hundred years, it says.

Father's mother says I'm my father's son, even though so many have me mistaken for his daughter.

One hundred years, to the day, if I am reading this correctly.

Press into pan.

Allow to rise.

Perhaps it is as bunk as mother's mother would say. Nothing can return magic to a family line once it's been lost. But I believe the prophecy is as genuine as my boyhood. Manhood. On the eve of my majority I

Score the dough with these runes.

And the back of one hand, with the same knife, with the same runes. Do not let the blood touch the dough—this is very important!

Bake.

Breathe.

Remove from heat. Allow to cool.

I grow impatient. The smell of warm bread, the tingle of possible magic. But I wait.

Slice with a clean athame.

Holding the slice in the rune-marked hand, take a bite.

This is your magic returning.

Allow to rise.

DUELING HEARTS

J.C. LOVERO (299 WORDS)

Daumyr Stormsorrow rose from the bed, drawn to the decanter of moonberry wine Prince Sigurd kept on his sideboard. He poured the deep purple—almost black—liquid into a crystal goblet etched with the royal family's crest. The aroma, dark and pungent, lifted his spirits.

He shrugged on the prince's oversized tunic, then climbed onto the balcony. Icy marble tickled his bare feet as he gazed into the starlit sky. A cruel winter painted the rolling hills in a layer of frost, like a dusting of powdered sugar.

If only their story could be so sweet. It started with a single look. A twinkle in the eye, then a stolen kiss in the shadows. Still, by daybreak, he would join the other dragons. Take up arms against the humans. The deeds of Sigurd's ancestors were ancient history, the perception of short-lived minds of men too limited to grasp.

Yet, after all these centuries, Daumyr still remembered the call to war as if it had happened only yesterday.

Before he could take flight, a pair of arms wrapped around him in a warm embrace.

"Come back to bed." Sigurd's words scaled his neck in a whisper.

Mouth agape, a single snowflake, delicate and white, landed on his cheek. Cool to the touch, it melted the swelling fire within him, reduced to a burning ember.

Though they had their roles to play, some battles were meant to be lost. In the morning, he would take to the skies, soaring above the clouds and disappearing into the purple sunrise to fulfill his destiny.

For now—in this moment—he wasn't Daumyr, leader of dragons; he was a man, madly in love. And while they danced under the protection of moonlight, he would keep his feet on the ground and surrender his heart.

GHOST INTO AIR

KAZY REED (296 WORDS)

Upon reaching adulthood, I had been chosen by the emperor as a benthru—a royal concubine destined for the governors on the outer planets. My soul died. Although my body had blossomed into that of a female, my mind and heart said otherwise. For many years, my family had accepted my choice to live as their son and brother. Now their lust for status had set their hearts against me.

"Come, Voya," Mother said. "It is an honor to be named as a benthru."

I looked at her in horror. "My name is Ganti. I am your son."

"Silence, foolish child," she growled. She thrust me at the emperor's guards and left me to my fate.

At the palace, my leather trousers and tunic, as well as my soul, were pulled roughly away. As the court maidens wrapped a form-fitting silk robe around my body, my eyes saw nothing. The long braid down my back—a style worn by all men in my family—was unwoven and the sleek black tresses were twisted into elaborate curls on my head. Sharp pins scraped my scalp and felt as though they pierced my heart. Thick, pale makeup removed all traces of my former self as it highlighted my feminine features.

In the mirror before me stood a ghost of whom I was meant to be.

After the maidens departed, I went to the window. Dusk approached, and I watched as a tansa bird lifted off the cool earth, rising to chase the warmth of the sun. I envied its freedom, its bravery, its strength against the harsh winds on its journey.

At that moment, I realized I could rise over my oppression. I removed the dainty sandals from my feet, climbed onto the balustrade, and stepped into air.

WINDFIRE KINGDOM
LYNDEN DALEY (295 WORDS)

Kyden was raised to be king, but he'd never felt like one. Men were supposed to be protectors. They were warriors and generals, weaponsmiths and watchmen. Most importantly, men commanded fire. And Kyden's lineage was the best. Their men manifested the wildest firestorms while their women called upon the swiftest winds. It's why they ruled.

Unfortunately, Kyden never managed a spark. And by the twin-gods, he'd tried.

A rapping sound drew his gaze to the window. He found his cousin, Makani, and rushed over to let her in.

"Makani? Did you climb the castle wall?"

"Nope," she replied. "Flew. My bedroom's barred."

"Oh, right." He frowned.

Makani was two years younger than him, but she already navigated the winds with ease. Although it was the last thing she wanted, she'd be named queen-heir soon. Managing a kingdom left little time for races, and all Makani wanted to do was fly.

Kyden had to admit, he saw the appeal of soaring away from his troubles.

"Don't look so sullen, your fire will come."

"I don't think it will. What if the twin-gods... made a mistake?"

"Impossible. Remember Great-Aunt Raelin? She was meant to be queen but couldn't call the wind. She became the best Battle-General of all time. Saved Windfire."

"But I... noticed something earlier. Watch." Kyden closed his eyes. A heartbeat later, the air stirred around them. It became a torrent.

Then Kyden rose.

Makani smiled proudly as he floated higher. Suddenly, he dropped back to the floor, face anguished.

"What... what am I?"

She grasped his hand. "You're my cousin, Kyden-Tadi Alrik. Don't you see? They made you this way on purpose. You're older, you'll take my place."

"But I... was raised to be king."

"Maybe so, but you were born to be queen."

FREE AT LAST

JOANNA MICHAL HOYT (297 WORDS)

Chloe stood atop the dam, listening for Geneva and looking down the valley. The Company's earthmovers below, poised to tear up the last of their town, looked almost beautiful iced with moonlight. The rusted mobile homes of the employees who'd refused to leave made a poorer showing—Chloe's and Geneva's was one of the dullest.

Geneva's voice crackled from the communicator Choe carried, tuned to the Company band all the workers had to listen to, announcing that terrorists had breached the dam and all personnel must evacuate immediately.

"Personnel" weren't too keen on the job anyway, knowing it could be their homes demolished next if the Company found anything mineable under them. Twelve battered trucks and vans peeled out.

Geneva said, "All out."

Chloe looked upstream and sang, soft and ragged, the song she'd first heard the water-woman singing, battering bruised arms against the dam. Other voices joined hers, wild voices rising, rising. The water-women, singing with terrifying beauty, with a strength Chloe had never heard.

Chloe pressed the switch, ran downstream. The earth shook. The roar rose almost as loud as the water-women's song as a great froth of water and sediment poured through the breach in the dam.

The women rose, colossal, twining in and out of one another, thundering down the valley. The earthmovers disappeared under their joined arms.

Those great arms gently lifted the trailer homes, each on its raft, bobbing higher and higher, every boat, for once, lifted by the rising tide.

Geneva spoke in Chloe's ear. "Our rowboat's here. Will they take us too?"

"Yes," Chloe said. "They keep their promises, same as we do." She climbed in with her wife, laughed and cried with her as the wild women carried them up over the valley and down toward the sea.

THE DUEL

NATHANIEL TAFF (294 WORDS)

The spell hit me like a giant's fist. Helpless, I was blasted high into the air to slam into the stone wall. Held in place by magic, I could only watch as High Sorcerer Leto rearranged his rumpled green robe, the only damage all my magic seemed to have done to him.

"Shameful," the man who had once been my master, my hero, sneered. "I was a fool to waste my time on you. And you are a fool to think that something like you can be anything less than a mistake."

With that, he broke his spell and I fell. My right leg buckled and cracked as I hit the floor and collapsed in a limp heap. With a final sniff of disdain, he turned on his heel and made briskly for the door, calling over his shoulder, "You can die here knowing you will never be anything, Marina. Not a real sorcerer, not a real man."

No, I thought as I lay broken in the rubble. If I was going to die here, it would be knowing what I am. No words of his could change that. Not even the name I had cast aside.

Wearily, I gripped my staff and pushed myself to my feet. Everything hurt. Blood ran down my scalp and into my eyes. My broken leg shook and threatened to topple me, but I was up. Summoning my last strength, I willed magic into my hand and let it build till I had the full power of a thunderstorm at my fingertips. Silver-white lightning flickered and danced between my fingertips as I made ready to let it go.

"I am a real sorcerer," I called as the lightning raced toward him. "And my name is Markus."

THE QUEEN OF BIRDS
AVERY VANDERLYLE (296 WORDS)

Every day Rav collected feathers: stuck in bushes, floating on ponds, pilfered from nests. Every evening, she stitched them together.

Her girlfriend, Thrush, watched her.

"Why are you making wings?" Thrush asked. "You won't be able to fly."

"The Queen of Birds will let me fly." Rav grinned, kissing her. "And then I'll marry you."

With every feather, Rav prayed to the Queen of Birds. With each needle that pricked her finger as she sewed. A little prayer for flight, a tiny gift of blood.

The wings were a visual cacophony, a riotous spread of speckled grays and browns, glossy black, blades of crimson, bands of white, a touch of blue.

On the summer solstice, the sun shone brilliant in an azure sky. Rav was ready.

She carried the wings up the mountain and unfurled them, staring down over the cliffside at her home below.

Rav fastened the wings around herself and tested the span. She bit her lip until she tasted blood and spat a final offering into the wind.

"Please, great Queen. Make these wings part of me."

A question floated in the air around her, soft as down and deadly as talons.

"I'm sure."

Rav's vision went white. She screamed; her shoulders burned as new muscles sprouted. But the wings were hers now. Instincts arose like song. The ebbs and flows of the wind were suddenly a language she could understand as if she'd been born with it.

She flew. Up, up, whooping in joy and gratitude. Then swooping lower, looking for Thrush who was jumping and waving, whooping, too.

"You did it!" Thrush cried as Rav darted around her. "Thank you, Queen of Birds!"

Rav echoed the words, grinning.

"One more question!" Thrush grinned back. "Who do you want at the wedding?"

SO HIGH UP WE'LL NEVER HEAR THEM SHOUTING

MEGHAN HYLAND (298 WORDS)

Winner - First Place

Dad leaves behind a duplex in the city, but Mom doesn't want to live there, and that's sad but okay. One day it's raining sideways outside and my friend Dena's parents kick her out. Her boyfriend won't take her in because he's afraid his friends will find out she's trans like me. So I give her the unit above mine.

Dena's like, "Thanks Ma!" and I'm like, "I'm not your Ma, Ma!" and we wrestle her furniture up the stairs, and I spy a crack in the landing wall. Turns out it's a door, and behind it another whole-ass stair, and then another whole-ass apartment.

Which makes zero sense until we meet Jamal and Fritz at the cafe. Nobody will rent them a place. We're like, "Come stay with us!" and they're like, "Hellz yeah!" and we move them in and surprise! Another crack, another stair, another apartment.

That unit goes to a family on the run from Tennessee, and the next one (turns out there's always a next one) to a mother and son fleeing Florida. I think, wait, don't buildings fall down when they get too tall? But we keep finding abandoned kids—from Idaho, from Indiana, from everywhere—and the house keeps growing, fifty states high and then some, until it looks like a tower of big ol' pizza boxes spiraling up through the clouds.

One day, Dena comes home crying. Her boyfriend's friends found her out, and he tried to take it out of her hide. I hold her like Mom used to hold me. Together we watch the rain fall sideways, and listen to the floors creak beneath the weight of friends we love like family, and outside, the storm throws itself against this house that rises up and up and never falls.

• • •

The judges loved this story — it scored high above its next competitor, a rarity in this contest. It's metaphorical and lyrical, well constructed — "brilliant, charming and affirming" in the words of one of the judges. Another called it the "ultimate queer communal home." A beautiful story we were honored to receive.

ABOUT QUEER SCI FI & OTHER WORLDS INK

Queer Sci Fi: We started QSF in 2014 as a place for writers and readers of LGBTQ+ spec fic—sci fi, fantasy, paranormal, horror and the like—to talk about their favorite books, share writing tips, and increase queer representation in romance and mainstream genre markets. Helmed by admins Scott, Angel, Ben and Ryane, QSF includes a blog, a vibrant FB discussion group, a twitter page, and an annual flash fiction contest that resulted in this book you are now reading.

Website: http://www.queerscifi.com
FB Discussion Group: facebook.com/groups/qsfdiscussions/
MeWe Discussion Group: https://mewe.com/group/
5c6c8bf7aef4005aa6bf3e12
Promo/News Page: facebook.com/queerscifi/
Twitter: Twitter.com/queerscifi/

Also by Queer Sci Fi:

Discovery (2016 - out of print)
Flight (2017 - out of print)
Renewal (2017 - out of print)
Impact (2018 - out of print)
Migration (2019 - out of print)
Innovation (2020 - out of print)
Ink (2021)
Clarity (2022)

Other Worlds Ink: The brainchild of J. Scott Coatsworth and his husband, Mark Guzman. OWI publishes Scott's works and the annual Queer Sci Fi flash fiction series and the Writers Save the World anthology series. We also create blog tours for authors, do eBook formatting and graphics work, and offer Wordpress site support for authors.

Printed in the USA
CPSIA information can be obtained
at www.ICGtesting.com
LVHW020226111123
763615LV00005B/44